Wes Gehring, a brilliant scribe of comedic fact, now turns his attention to wonderful mysterious laugh out-loud fiction story telling. Gehring's fast-paced dry sense of humor is delightful as we try to solve this sidesplitting murder mystery. If you absolutely hate stuffy academic types, you will treasure this book.

Jim Shasky, Emmy winning director.

"Up to now, readers have known Wes Gehring only through his insightful, brilliant nonfiction works on the history of movies. But as his new nourish foray into the seamy world of cold-blooded murder and tenured professorship proves, Wes is more, much more."

Rod Richey, *Los Angeles Daily News*

THE
CHARLIE CHAPLIN MURDER MYSTERY

(a comic novel)

by

Wes D. Gehring

RAMBLE HOUSE

ISBN 0-9774527-1-9

RAMBLE HOUSE

www.ramblehouse.com
fender@ramblehouse.com

To Sarah & Emily and the regular readers of my books, plus even those who are *irregular* but coping. . .

Charlie's Revolving Door

In Chaplin's *The Cure*
Charlie enters but can't
Escape a revolving door:

Too fast
Now past
Too fast
Now past
Too fast
Now past

And amidst the fun is
Another Charlie metaphor
For life.

—Wes D. Gehring

INTRODUCTION

Following in the footsteps of Stuart Kaminsky, Wes Gehring is a
college professor who has decided to try his hand at the writing of a
mystery novel. Like Kaminsky, Gehring utilizes an area with which
he is most familiar, namely the history of film comedy. Unlike
Kaminsky, he does not set his novel in the past with a fictional private
detective, like Toby Peters, but rather writes of the present and of a
hero who reads remarkably like a college professor named Wes
Gehring.

Only his students will know how much of Wes is to be found in
David Caine or how much Middletown University resembles the author's own Ball State University. Those familiar with the author's
considerable writings on all aspects and all types of practitioners of
film comedy will know that the motion picture-related background
can only be covered in style and with wry humor.

I am not giving away too much of the plot when I reveal that the
murder, and subsequent mayhem, revolves around a lost Charlie
Chaplin film. In reality, apart from SEA GULLS, directed by Josef
von Sternberg, starring leading lady Edna Purviance and financed by
the comedian, there are no "lost" Chaplin features or short subjects.
Of all comedians from the silent era, Chaplin is the one whose films,
outtakes, screen tests and abortive projects have survived pretty much
intact.

And that is in large part thanks to his last wife Oona, who returned
to the United States after her husband was barred from re-entry in
1952 and shipped what she could back to the safety of Europe and its
more democratic and liberal environment.

Oona O'Neill Chaplin was the last in a long line of wives, mis-
tresses and lovers. According to Chaplin, she was the best; and she
was most certainly the one best equipped to love and cherish him in
old age. It is an earlier Chaplin wife, one about whom one does not
read too much, who plays a crucial, if no longer active, role in THE
CHARLIE CHAPLIN MURDER MYSTERY. And it is a most unusual film project in which she was to star opposite Chaplin that is
integral to the storyline.

Wes Gehring's skills as both a novelist and a historian are com-
bined as he writes of this lost Chaplin film, creating a scenario that is
original and yet very much in the Chaplin style. It is influenced by

other Chaplin screenplays and performances, and yet it is unique. It is almost as if he is able to read Chaplin's mind and fully to comprehend his artistic temperament. Gehring's ploy is as audacious as the Chaplin film that he creates.

THE CHARLIE CHAPLIN MURDER MYSTERY is firmly grounded in the past and in the golden age of the movies. At the same time, it provides a cheery and entertaining study of the current academic scene. And what could be more cheery than the murder of a college professor, no matter how well liked or well versed in the arcana of film history?

—Anthony Slide

Anthony Slide is the author or editor of more than sixty books on the history of popular entertainment, and the editor of the "filmmakers" series, published by Scarecrow Press. Two of his works, *The American Film Industry: A Historical Dictionary* and *The Encyclopedia of Vaudeville*, have been named outstanding reference sources of the year by the American Library Association. In 1990, in recognition of his work in the field, he received a honorary doctorate of letters from Bowling Green, at which time he was hailed by legendary early movie actress Lillian Gish as "our preeminent historian of the silent film".

Credit Acknowledgement:

This novel contains brief quotes from both Chaplin's *My Trip Abroad* (1922) and *My Autobiography* (1964), and Lita Grey Chaplin's *My Life With Chaplin* (1966). Now defunct period newspapers were also an occasional source. The preparation of this novel was greatly assisted by Sarah & Emily Gehring, Kathy Huggler, Matt Clemens, Janet Warrner, and Jean Thurman. And a special thank you goes to my parents, with my dad first encouraging me to write a novel.

On the Characters:

Other than the occasional inclusion of historic film figures, any similarities between actual people, living or dead, are purely coincidental and merit no cracks about a lack of imagination on the author's part. Cain and his supporting players are all made up, like in the movies.

You haven't seen enough movies. All of life's riddles are answered in the movies.

—Davis *(Steve Martin) in* Grand Canyon *(1991)*

THE
CHARLIE CHAPLIN
MURDER
MYSTERY

Chapter 1

So many people have claimed to have given Chaplin his start that film historian Terry Ramsaye was moved to observe: "The original discovers of Charlie Chaplin should form an association and hold a convention at the Polo Grounds, if the seating facilities are adequate."

My image of humanity was not very high that Friday night in October. I'd just returned from one of those all-you-can-eat buffets. Talk about scary people. We're dealing with folks so big that a snapshot would necessitate aerial photography. But my criteria for disappointment in the species was about to take a new slant.

Back at my apartment I had papers to correct. I'm David Caine, a forty-five year old film professor at Middletown University, a large state college in Middletown, Indiana. I'm a nationally known authority on American film comedy, and the author of sixteen books on various entertainers and comic genres. Writing defines me; teaching is the day job. Consistent with that, I was looking for excuses not to correct papers. I found one when I turned on the TV and caught a news bulletin. One of my teaching colleagues, Evert Harris, had been brutally murdered at his home. I was in knee shaking shock. I knew Harris well; why would anyone want to murder harmless old Ev? Ironically, he loved a good mystery. Now he was one.

Higher education hates to lose teachers in this fashion; they'd prefer to whittle the ranks down through low salaries and meager benefits. On the plus side, murder does represent a provocative way to thin out the tenure density (read: dead wood) of many universities.

In this case, however, I didn't think it was an academic hit squad. Because Evert was an internationally respected expert on silent film, and the cinema department's only endowed chair. More precisely, he was the (cue the Hallelujah Chorus) "Joseph P. Tracy Professor of the Humanities." See, an endowed university chair is where a fat cat gives a major piece of change (million bucks minimum) to have his name forever associated with a lofty and poetic endeavor. (In this case, Evert's work on early film.) Ironically, this is in direct contrast to the nefarious manner in which the money was often acquired. Thus, you could say that Evert's endowed chair was yet another example of academic moneylaundering. Yes, if you lift up this cheery rock (endowments) of academia you're bound to find wormy things slithering for cover.

Harris was one old professor. But then most endowed chairs (and other assorted academic furniture) are ancient. And he dressed like he had just slipped out of a 1920s time capsule, including starched white shirts with cuff links, and an exciting selection of bow ties. Still, he had this endearing habit of playing the octogenarian class clown. When he disliked a movie he might observe, "The picture needs a certain something. . .possibly burial." Now he was the one in need of planting.

Harris had written over three dozen film related books, with silent movie actress Mary Pickford once calling him "the historian who understands us best." But what I liked about his writing was that he never lost sight of the lesser lights. That is, while he would often chronicle the name personalities (like the Pickfords), who were served by an army of biographers, he reminded readers that the movies were a collaborative art form made possible by countless men and women who would never have biographers.

So why kill this distinguished old man? Well, he was loaded. Money is always a popular incentive for murder. Moreover, Evert always carried tons of cash, which he called his "mad money." Evert didn't believe in credit cards. As a corollary to the wealth, Harris' home was filled with priceless movie memorabilia, from original posters to autographed scripts and actual props. One of his special film toys was *the* Maltese Falcon statue used in the Bogart detective classic of the same name. Personally, I really loved the old man, except for his paranoia. Everything was a conspiracy with Evert; and I never bought into it, until now

Using plain old hate as a motive for murder was plausible, I suppose. Evert could be an elitist shmuck with untenured faculty and students. Plus, many overworked junior instructors were steamed about Harris' light teaching load and the generous travel stipend he received — both perks of the average chair everywhere. In contrast, the untenured often paid for research trips out-of-pocket, and taught the boringly overcrowded core classes. From that vantage point, I suppose there were several young instructors who, like in the film *Murder on the Orient Express*, might have collaborated on a killing. Still, unless Charlie Chaplin and Buster Keaton really piss you off (Harris' area of expertise), I didn't see this being done by a department death squad.

I learned more about Evert's demise the next day when a university friend, Mark Roberts, called. It turned out that he found the body. They had been working on an article together and Mark was dropping off some books for Evert to peruse over the weekend. Their topic: silent film sex symbols. This didn't surprise me since Mark was the most sex-obsessed person I knew — we all described him as tall, dark, and horny. He appeared forty, funny, and twisted — but in a good way. He resembled a younger Jack Nicholson (circa *The Last Detail*), and even had Jack's hydraulic eyebrow action going on — to punctuate his propensity for ribald comments.

Mark told me Evert's front door had been wide open. A DVD of Chaplin's movie *The Gold Rush* had been playing on the TV. Mark found the comedian's voice-over narration especially creepy to listen to as he explored a ransacked house. Like a stereotypical professor, Evert turned up in the library, still holding a copy of Chaplin's autobiography. (One might say Harris belonged to the denomination of Charlie, where you regularly genuflect towards a little man with east west feet, baggy pants, and a cane.)

In life the old man's crinkly eyes were so deeply set they could have been peeking out directly from the recesses of his brain. But this time, according to Mark, you could actually see the brains, too, courtesy of a heavy handed murderer. Talking a mile a minute, Mark said, "Can you believe someone bludgeoned Evert to death with his Maltese Falcon statue? Unfucking believable! And there was his damn cat [Ballou] licking away at the old guy's grey matter like it was free day at the fish market. I hate cats. Then I heard this scream and performed a Chuck Yeager out of the house. We're talkin' vapor trails here. Only later did I realize that I was the one that screamed.

At this point Mark started to lose it on the phone and I told him to calm down and I'd be right over. We'd bonded a couple years before when our divorces had overlapped — his fourth and my third. Coincidently, both marriages ended because of religious differences, we were Methodist, and they were satanic. These unions had been like hell, without the frills.

I found Mark chain-smoking on his frontporch, seemingly calmer but with a pasty white tone to his complexion. "How's it going, buddy?" was all I could think to say. I'm really slick in stressful situations.

"Oh, I'm doing better now that I'm back in denial. Sorry to make you come over. But I appreciate it. I just started seeing poor Evert. . ."

"It must have been horrible."

While his eye hinted at the pain, he worked hard to stay focused. Taking an especially long drag on his cigarette he suddenly volunteered, "You know, the funny thing is, after I phoned the police from a neighbor's house, I went back in."

"Why?"

"I just kept thinking of that damn cat. . .I chased it out, and covered Evert up. . .used a doily off an end table."

"You're a class act, Mark."

"The strange thing, when I was covering him up, I noticed that he had scribbled the names Chaplin and Jesus repeatedly on a piece of paper. What d'you make of that?"

"Well, I think we can safely eliminate them as suspects."

Laughing, Mark affectionately said, "You're a sick man, David."

"Nope, just using dark comedy to cope."

"Okay, so we've heard from Caine the comedy therapist. What does your professorial side have to say?"

"Well, back in the 1920s Chaplin claimed his movie alter ego, the Tramp, was more popular than Christ," I said.

"No shit. I thought just John Lennon had made that unfortunate analogy."

"Chaplin screwed up, too."

"So what happened? Did the public trash his merchandise, like they did with the Beatles?"

"No, Chaplin was much better at damage control."

"Interesting. Not necessarily relevant but the next time I'm on *Jeopardy* maybe I can use it."

"Seriously, the Chaplin-Christ connection seems to ring a bell. I want to look into it," I said, as Mark lit up another cigarette.

I let him chatter on for a while. He's always in the moment, but it's not always going to be the moment you're in. Still, I figured his long-windedness was an outgrowth of finding Professor Harris oozingly dead. When I tuned Mark back in he was saying, "Of course, I can be had for a song, or maybe a short medley." My laughter validated his riff, and before leaving we made plans to tip a few the next day, following the university's memorial service for Evert.

Back at my apartment I pulled out my latest writing project, an article on film noir, the genre that made Bogart tough guy royalty. But my mind kept wandering back to Evert's ventilated head and the curious coupling by the dead man of the names Chaplin and Jesus. What would Bogie do in a spot like this? I imitated his half smile, where only the lower lip moves. A little saliva rolled down my chin. . .Booze. I needed some liquid fun.

Once fortified with spirits, which sounds a bit mystical, I went to my book shelves and pulled down a criticism text I'd written on Chaplin fresh out of grad school, back when the world was young. My memory of the text should have been better, but I'd written so much since then. And sadly, one forgets. But I turned a few pages and bingo, I was on to something. Back in the 1920s Chaplin had briefly flirted with playing Christ in a straight film drama. How this tied into Evert's murder I didn't know. But it was a start.

The next day I took in the university's memorial send-off for one of their own. Mark and I sat in the back and tried not to get into trouble. Serious situation or not, some friendships take you back to class-clown days, and this was one of them. But neither of us got any detention, or anything. The whole thing reminded me of that Chuckles the Clown funeral episode of the *Mary Tyler Moore Show*, where her case of the giggles escalates into all-out laughter. Mark and I didn't exactly go there but it was close. Of course, it didn't help that at one point Mark leaned over and shared a limerick from his ever expanding collection:

> Have you heard of the Bishop of Kew
> Who preached with his vestments askew?
> A lady named Morgan
> Caught sight of his organ,
> And fainted away in her pew.

He then topped this off with some Nicholsonesque eyebrow raising.

Luckily, there wasn't a lot of "It's God's will" statements thrown around by the presiding clergyman. When that happens, it always seems to imply that He is just plain mean spirited, à la, "Well, this year we'll be signing up for the Black Plague, with an option on famine to buy, and oh yes, let's put the Spanish Inquisition on lay-away." But I won't go on.

The service for Evert also featured several short talks by untenured colleagues trying for brownie points with the dean, and by three graduate students hoping to curry favor within the department politics (which passes for Ph.D. study). Sadly, all but one of the testimonials were so bland you wanted to pour A-1 on them. The exception was from a student who normally had all the emotional stability of a parrot. But on this occasion she was, to borrow a line from Stuart Scott, "As cool as the other side of the pillow." Her comments played as sincerely heartfelt, and for the first time I was feeling the classic funeral-time blues. You know, like you're only moments away from recording a country album.

At this precise second Mark nudged me and redirected my gaze from the former Fleety Belle student, to a femme fatale type who'd just sat down near the back of the university chapel. She reminded me of the leggy Cyd Charisse in the noirish fantasy from the 50's film *Singin' in the Rain*. It was the sort of image that makes a guy's teeth sweat, followed by choking on his Ju-Ju-Bees. To borrow a line from Woody Allen, "She could have caused cardiac arrest in a yak."

"What?" I said. Mark had whispered something to me, but sexy visuals tend to shut down my auditory reception and I had to ask him to repeat.

"I said, 'she was all over Evert last week in his office.'"

"What is she, nearsighted? The man could have been her grand-daddy."

"Who's your daddy?"

"Shut-up Mark. People will think you're a moron."

"Yes, and we're organized."

By now the ceremony was breaking up, and as we exited the chapel our mystery lady slipped into a dark-colored Buick. What made the image especially memorable was that the guy holding the door, honest to God (I couldn't believe it), was a dwarf in a bright yellow suit. It looked like he'd just come from the *Wizard of Oz* cast party. I half expected to see Toto and some flying monkeys.

With a nod towards the dwarf, I told Mark, "I don't think we're in Kansas anymore."

While watching the little fellow close the door behind her, and then join the driver in the front, Mark casually replied, "You know, if they remade *The Wizard of Oz* today there'd be a high speed car chase on the Yellow Brick Road, and gratuitous sex. . .probably with Munchkins."

Getting into the spirit of things by assuming a Dorothy-like voice, I added, "Oh, I could never leave Kansas and its inspired flatness again. Where else can I watch Toto run away [pause] for three weeks?"

We walked to a nearby bar for our own postmortem on why Evert had taken a dirt nap. Playing to its largely academic cliental, the bar was called *The Library*, with even a commemorative plaque to Frederick Exley, who once frequented the place the semester he guest lectured at Middletown University. Sadly, his heavy drinking led to an early checkout — a frequent fate of writers who merit tavern plaques.

Keeping our priorities in order, we immediately ordered a pitcher of beer. Alcohol doesn't solve problems but it does reduce their size.

A mutual friend came by the booth just then and nearly collided with our retreating waitress. "Drunk?" I said.

"No. But what a lovely idea," was his response as he sailed by.

As Mark and I settled in for our own drinking tutorial he asked if I'd done my homework on Chaplin and Jesus.

"Yes, oh oversexed one. It seems that our comedian had plans to ditch the derby and do the crown of thorns thing."

"Alright, now we're cooking. So what happened then, Bogie?"

"Well, that seems to be it. He never played Jesus, probably because lots of people were steamed when he even pretended to be a minister in *The Pilgrim*."

"When was this? And how pissed did they get?"

"It was the early 1920's and the picture was banned in several areas, including much of Pennsylvania."

"You're joking."

"No, if I were joking, I would have said, 'How many Mennonites does it take to screw in a light bulb? [pause] It doesn't make any difference, because they will all surely burn in hell.'" Mark laughed and I returned to my regularly scheduled answer. "Chaplin wasn't quite so universally acclaimed back then. A Tramp who lifted women's skirts with his cane, kicked authority figures in the keister, and just generally raised hell bothered blue nose America."

"Sounds like my kind of guy."

"And that says nothing about Chuck's controversial personal life, the left wing politics and all the young women."

"Yes, I told you, he's the man. Of course, this doesn't get us any closer to why Evert was scribbling "Chaplin" and "Jesus" before he bought the farm."

"Unless," I said.

"Unless what?"

"Try this on. What if Chaplin did shoot some "Jesus" footage? Not a whole movie, mind you, just some test film. Maybe a shuffling Christ skidding around a corner, or Jesus kicking the shit out of the moneylenders."

"That would be worth major bucks," Mark said excitedly. "Right?"

"You couldn't count high enough."

"Enough to kill for?"

"Are you kidding? Serious film collectors are worse than piranhas at lunch time. Anything goes."

"Oh, come on."

"Oh, yeah. A few years ago a prominent West coast collector was found on a meat hook in his own walk-in freezer. Needless to say, all of his films were gone, and there was nothing in that collection remotely as valuable as the possibility of Charlie Chaplin tap dancing through Christ's story. Damn, imagine Chuck on the cross. I might kill for that myself."

Mark pulled back in mock horror and said in that melodious voice of his, "Stop, you're scaring me."

"The point is, there's just no record of Chaplin doing anything like that."

"Maybe we should have a film comedy séance and see if we can conjure up a message from Chaplin, or the late great Professor Harris."

"You bring the Quija board and I'll bring the candles."

We laughed and decided to order some food, in case we hadn't eaten. But in less than twenty-four hours I would, indeed, receive a message from the victim, not to mention a visit from a dwarf with a penchant for yellow. I was about to become a player in a murder mystery.

Chapter 2

During World War I, English children sang the "Charlie Chaplin" song set to the music of "Gentle Jesus":

> *"Charlie Chaplin meek and mild*
> *Took a sausage from a child.*
> *When the child began to cry*
> *Charlie slapped him in the eye."*

For once I was in early on a Monday. Lucky me, I ran into a media circus. By now the national news agencies had picked up on the comic irony of a prominent film historian buying it with a Maltese Falcon to the head. There was a regular conga line of reporters, everyone from *USA Today* to *CNN* was hanging out on campus that morning. And with Evert being from our department, we were at ground zero. It's hard to keep the lid on a juicy demise like Evert's. Dr. Charles, the film department chairman, was holding a mini-press conference in his office when I came in. Ah, the joys of leadership. They were converging on him like animals at a waterhole.

Before seeking sanctuary in my office, I went by the mail room and picked up the never ending load of trash that passes for campus correspondence and snail mail. I grabbed the whole formidable stack and went back to my home-away-from home. Going into my office never failed to relax me, because it was full of all the things that make me want to get up in the morning — pictures of my daughters (made all the more special by divorce guilt, for which I'm the Midwest distributor), several million books, and numerous framed original film posters. I was a sucker for movie memorabilia. I guess that was another thing that Evert and I connected on.

Oh, and I should mention the old Philco wooden console floor model radio I had. It was a great ice breaker with students, not to mention how much Mark enjoyed working all the knobs. He loved the incongruity of tuning in something like the Rolling Stones' "Jumpin' Jack Flash" on a 1930s radio.

What was decidedly missing were any pictures of a sweetheart. I had retired for the time being from the relationship game. The last Mrs. Caine, or as she was known in the *Bible*, the Antichrist, had really done a number on me. But my hat's off to people who have a working relationship.

Of course, I still felt that women were more into commitment control. From my warped mid-forties perspective, I'd say men don't commit. If anything, they ultimately just surrender.

Anyway, I sat down and started the mail opening process. Since I hadn't been in since Thursday (no Friday classes), half a week's worth of mail had piled up. After I had "round filed" several items, I came to a large bulky padded envelope with a law firm for a return address. Bigger is seldom better, especially with lawyers, but it had me mildly interested. My curiosity increased further when I thought I recognized old Evert's handwriting in the scrawl that passed for my name on the envelope. What the hell could it be?

"It" turned out to be a film poster, brittle with age, folded into the standard rectangular shape (roughly a foot by ten inches) for what was called a full-sheet (a poster approximately 30 by 40 inches in size). It appeared to have been not opened, or unfolded, for years. But what was it?

I gingerly laid it on the carpeted floor and ever so carefully worked with the fragile creases, slowly laboring towards full display mode. Like Joe Archivist, it took me several minutes to completely unfold the poster. And when I backed off for a better view I had to rub my eyes. I couldn't be seeing what I was seeing. Suddenly I was having difficulty breathing, like the time I recovered a fumble in high school football and found myself at the bottom of the world's largest pile of pituitary cases.

Despite being a prof who normally keeps his office door open to encourage students to come and talk, at this point I quickly shut myself off. And then I hastily turned back to the poster, half convinced it wouldn't be there. . .that I had imagined everything. But I wasn't off my nut. There it was in all its glory — a Chaplin poster for a Christ picture undocumented in any film history! I felt faint, and I never feel faint.

There were two full-figure Al Hirschfeld-like drawings on the poster. The first was of Chaplin in his signature Charlie the Tramp costume caught in mid-strut, one hand jauntily holding his cane, the other securing the derby. Directly behind him, like a shadow, was a Christ-like form in flowing robes. But the facial features of the latter figure were definitely those of Chaplin. That fact was further underlined with the poster's slogan — "Chaplin's 2 Greatest Roles. . .In One Movie!" And the film's title helped explain the Biblical connection — *Charlie and the Time Machine.*

Contrary to the popular misconception that older posters are not as colorful as their contemporary counterparts, this Chaplin full-sheet was bright and beautiful. The black line-drawn figures stood out on the parchment colored paper, with vivid burnt orange lettering for the title, and an intense yellow for the slogan. The Hirschfeld-like drawings gave the Chaplin figures an exuberance and style one would wish for one's self. The comedian's alter ego (times two) had never looked so inspired. For the longest time I just stood there feasting my eyes on this treasure, lost in a strange feeling of absolute harmony.

Only after I had savored the moment for many moments did I start to return to reality, a condition which I feel is extremely overrated. Why had Evert sent this to me? Looking back in the envelope I found a letter. If this were a film, there would now be that eerie beyond-the-grave type soundtrack music, with the actual voice of the victim reading his own letter. But since this is a low-budget story, you'll just have to handle the job yourself, and please try to avoid moving your lips:

David —

If you're reading this the clock has already struck midnight for me. Don't pity the old professor, I've lived through most of life's storms and seldom got wet. I'm gifting you with this because I know you'll give it a good home, and I really enjoyed your Chaplin biography. Did I ever tell you that?

Be on your toes, however, about this poster. Tell no one. Only a handful know of its existence, but they would stop at nothing to get it.

Remember my fascination with games and puzzles? Would you accept a challenge from a dead man — sort of a movie sequel idea? If you decide to play, and play well, I can promise you the inside track on one whale of a story concerning *Charlie and the Time Machine.* Your first task is to find the lock for the enclosed key.

[Key? I picked up the large seemingly empty envelope and turned the open end down. A small rust colored key fell silently to the carpet.]

And David, whether you join this adventure or not, take care of yourself, enjoy the poster, and don't think of me as dead. I'd rather you thought of my favorite movie title as my closing comment, *Went to Coney Island On A Mission From God. . .Be Back By Five.*

Evert

Just as I finished reading the letter there was a knock on my door and I uncorked a vertical jump of All-American proportions. I could've been more frightened but it would've taken a visit from "Hannibal the Cannibal" Lecter, Norman Bates, and the boogeyman of your choice. Fittingly, when I asked through the door who it was, my voice came out in a squeaky Barney Fife tone.

"You suckin' helium again, Pop?" It was my youngest daughter, Holly, the professional smart aleck — a pretty, dark haired cutup, with big brown eyes. She was a freshman at the university and already a member of the school's celebrated improv group — "Duck's Breath Theatre, or Full Frontal Comedy." She even used some Chaplin schtick for her "Duck Breath" audition. We shared a love of movies, baseball, and hot fudge sundaes, though there were all those "loan" requests. Having a teenager is like living with the homeless — "Can I have a dollar?"

I opened the door, motioned her in, and quietly said, "Boy, have I got a surprise for you."

"First of all, 'Boy' is highly inaccurate, and secondly, that's gonna cost ya."

With fatherly affection I said, "Sweetie, get in here, shut the door and take a look at my 'surprise' down there."

"Super! You got another poster? For me?"

I ignored that ludicrous presumption on her part, and watched her examine the poster. Her face suddenly took on an incredulous expression and she let out a low whistle. "Chaplin never made *Charlie and the Time Machine. . .did* he?"

"Not as far as I know. But the extent of what I know just might have taken a major hit."

"Where the hell did you get this? It must have cost a fortune. Have you gotten into my trust fund again?"

"Honey, it would probably be in your best interest if I didn't spill the beans."

"Forget that angle, Dad. No film secrets in this family."

"But this isn't normal."

"Yeah, like our family wrote the book on normal."

"Okay, but this involves a murder."

"So, who'd you kill for this thing?"

"Thanks. . .it's nice to know I'm still your hero. I got it in the mail, smart aleck. It's a gift from our recently murdered Professor Evert. And I can't help thinking there's some connection between the poster and his death."

"How do you mean?"

"He sent me a challenge with the poster gift."

"Wait a minute. I'm confused. The dead man sent you what?" I handed Holly the letter and she shook her head as she read it. "Go-for-it Dad!" Then she read it again. "So what's the key look like?" Giving the key a cursory look, Holly said, "It doesn't look like anything special, not like this poster."

Lost in thought I added, "I can't believe how well Evert read me."

"Because Chaplin is God," she said as much to herself as me.

"Bless your heart. You remembered that lecture. . .I'd do just about anything, even with risks, to find out more about *Charlie and the Time Machine*. But there might not be any connection between the poster and Evert's death."

Holly's gaze returned to the poster, and she said, "It's lovely. Do you think Chaplin actually shot the film?"

"I don't know how it could have been kept under wraps all these years. . .but yesterday I wouldn't have believed any poster art for it existed, either." I worried that this might be the lead car in a long train of things I didn't know.

"When would you date this from?" Holly had read all my books and had sat in on my classes well before getting to college. She was definitely up on her Chaplin.

"Sometime in the early 1920s. The poster's back-to-back figures are not unlike some art work for *The Kid* in 1921, where Jackie Coogan is a carbon copy of Chaplin's Charlie the Tramp. Plus, now that I think about it, there's a drawing of Christ used early in that film, where He's made to carry the cross."

"You're good Pop, a regular human highlight machine." Smiling, she added, "But then that's why you get the big bucks."

"Yeah, right. You know, the other thing that connects it to this time frame is Chaplin's *The Idle Class*. It's the same year as *The Kid*, and he plays two parts. Maybe that was the catalyst for two roles in *Charlie and the Time Machine*."

Suddenly Holly got this huge grin on her face, and became more than a little animated, like the grade school child bursting with an answer, "Dad, you're gonna like this. I've got another period link for you. And a thank you isn't even necessary. A simple hallelujah will suffice."

"I'm all ears."

"Well, besides that, didn't Chaplin also meet H. G. Wells in 1921?"

"You're right, for the London premiere of *The Kid*. There's our *Time Machine* connection. Way to go Holly! Do I see some kick ass quiz show in your future?"

"Before you start booking my flight to New York, let me see that key again, Pop."

"Sure, be my guest. But it could be to anything, from a little tin box under his bed, to his boyhood bicycle chain. It'll be a real crap shoot to figure out." Holly examined it intently, turning it over in her hand several times. "Well, what's the verdict, Nancy Drew?" I asked.

"You know, I think Mrs. Franklin has one just like that. Or, at least she did, when I had her in 9th grade." Holly's former high school just happened to be part of the college campus, and was located only four blocks away.

"Don't kid a kidder. Are you sure?"

"Well, I'm not a locksmith, Pop, but it sure looks like the key Franklin wore around her neck. She was always playing with it while she talked."

"Is Franklin the one they used to describe as having 'a wit so dry [Holly joined in] you wonder where she kept the olive.' I'll take that as a yes."

"I hope she's still with us. She was as old as dirt when I had her, and that's been a while."

Looking Franklin up in the campus directory, I breathed a sigh of relief, "She's still listed as an instructor."

Getting a mischievous expression on her face Holly observed, "You know Pop, if you're really serious about this, I need to get you a few things."

"Such as?"

"Well, as a budding private eye you really need a ratty old trench coat, and [starting to open my desk drawers] where's that half empty bottle of Scotch? You need some broken Venetian blinds at the window, and some sort of blinking neon light just outside."

"I'll get university maintenance right on it," I said.

"Oh, and you need a single dim-lit lamp on the desk and an ashtray with lots of lipstick-stained cigarettes."

"It's a smoke-free university — I'll just settle for the well-stacked doll with tears in her eyes waiting up for me in my office." As we both laughed I carefully folded up the Charlie poster.

"So what happens next?"

Pocketing the key, I respond, "I'll hold onto this but *Charlie and the Time Machine* best be put away. It's going in our special security spot." And as if on cue, Holly lifted a framed full-sheet poster of Chaplin's *Modern Times* off the wall, revealing a small built-in opening where there had once been a phone. It now doubled as my low-tech safe. The *Time Machine* poster now joined a box of old baseball cards, and the *Modern Times* cover was soon back up.

"What's our next move?"

"*Our* move? In the history of bad ideas that would be a humdinger."

"Yeah, right."

"Do you have a room temperature I.Q.? I won't take a chance on you ending up with a ventilated noodle."

"But it's okay for you? Oh, come on, Dad. You need me and you know it. I'll be the lookout. And I did solve the key puzzle already."

"That remains to be seen," I answered.

"At least think about it."

"Only if you could conduct your gumshoe activity from some safe parallel universe."

"Speaking of parallel universes, what time is it?"

Looking at my watch I half shout, "Sweet Jesus, we need to haul ass!" As we rush to class I vaguely worry about the Yellow Brick Road Evert's game has pointed me (and no doubt Holly) towards.

Chapter 3

After watching the eloquent grace of Chaplin in the 1917 short film Easy Street, *W. C. Fields was asked what he thought of the comedian's performance. The jealous Fields snapped, "He's the world's greatest ballet dancer, and if I ever meet the son of a bitch I'll murder him."*

My getting to class a little late was never a problem for my students. But trying to get *them* to stay a few extra minutes, now there was a problem, except for Holly (who was also in this particular class). But thanks to my daughter's reminder, we were merely fashionably late, and I wouldn't be requesting any extra class time. The lecture subject was an examination of film noir, the genre of down and out detectives.

Ironically, this film genre was becoming a reality for me. Don't get me wrong, I was definitely *not* in the tough guy Bogart/Philip Marlow tradition of the 1946 *Big Sleep*. I'm still essentially a live action version of Charlie Brown. Yet, I very much related to the most basic differences between the traditional detective, à la Sherlock Holmes, and the noir private eye. Whereas Sherlock could deduct a million facts from something as simple as a footprint ("he had sixty-six cents in his pocket and a mole on his right buttock," he'd say), the noir dick is just scrambling to stay ahead of the audience. Think of Jack Nicholson in *Chinatown*. At times, he's dumber than a *bag of hammers*. Never call an undersized mobster a "midget." Roman Polanski, in a cameo, darn near cuts off Jack's nose as payback.

At one point during my lecture I could have sworn I saw a small yellow blur lurking outside the classroom door. But given all that had transpired, and my film noir lecture, it seemed like I was having some sort of movie-cum-funeral flashback. Or, maybe it was just yesterday's shellfish . . . .

After class, there were a handful of questions ranging from paper due dates to whether I preferred Bogart as Sam Spade, or as Marlowe. They were a good bunch of students, and not a smart ass in the bunch, though Holly would occasionally hit me with some affectionate heckling. Normally, she would hang out with me some more after class, too. But on Mondays she had back-to-back lectures, which only gave her time for a wave to Dad and a quick exit.

It was just as well, given the nature of my afternoon visitor. During my lecture I had been suffering from neither a flashback nor a shellfish reaction. The dwarf from the funeral was on to me. Maybe two minutes after I'd returned to my office, there was a knock on my half-open door. It was the little man in yellow.

Where were all those students who normally follow me back to my office with additional questions, or just to shoot the shit? Great, they leave me alone with Peter Lorre's grandson.

Despite his bargain basement size, he seemed formidable, like a fire plug with attitude. Even his face had muscles. And while his suit was canary yellow, it was tailor-made, and he wore it with confidence — a lot of confidence. There was not a chance I would call him a "midget."

My "come in" response to his knock brought him into the doorway but he seemed reluctant to either move further, or say anything. Instead, he methodically surveyed my office like he'd come to sublet the place, or price the items for an auction.

I think I keep a pretty tidy office. But the minute somebody starts to eyeball it like that, the place seems to take on the appearance, even to me, of that dump in *Deliverance*, where Georgia backwoods types have been in-breeding and cooking possum for years. But if you haven't seen this, you've missed a funny analogy, and it serves you right. (Draw what you want from this, but keep it to one side of the page please. And not a word about the "Dueling Banjos" scene.)

Anyway, part of me wanted to pistol whip the little shit and grind him up for mulch. But this shrimp's presence was somehow threatening, and I didn't go there. Suddenly an old Flip Wilson routine came to mind, where he said, "I don't trust midgets. A midget bit my uncle once. You know, they don't come up any higher than here [Flip lightly touches his crotch area]."

The smile generated by this Wilson memory seemed to startle the dwarf at my door, a phrase which could also double as the title of a midget love song. It was like my smile had inadvertently made him blink in a staring contest. But maybe munchkins are easily rattled. I flirted with saying, "How're things in Oz?" or "What's the word from

Dorothy?" but thought better of it. Ultimately, I went with the ever popular, user-friendly, "Can I help you?" (Mom was a bear for politeness.)

"You Professor Caine?" He had a big melodious voice for such a small fellow, like an economy sized Orson Welles. . .a walking boom box.

"Who wants to know?" I'd always wanted to say that.

"Let's just say I'm the man with no name, like Clint Eastwood's character in those spaghetti westerns. Yeah, like Clint. Some joke, huh?"

"I've never had it so good."

"Ah, a happy solution then." Closing the door he added, "I'd like to ask you some questions." With that he climbed up in one of my office chairs, his little legs dangling a foot off the ground. I didn't know whether to be afraid, or burp him. I was about to be interrogated by a thumb-sized thug. What was the politically correct phrase, vertically-challenged hood? Or how about the original *Little Caesar*, or the real Baby Face Nelson?

However, I avoided controversy entirely, and asked, "So what do you want to know, Blondie?"

"Blondie?"

"That's what Clint really went by in the best of the spaghetti westerns — *The Good, the Bad, and the Ugly*."

"Yes, of course, right you are, Herr Professor. I need to talk to you about your friend Evert. Did he ever give you anything?"

"Flowers, occasionally candy, and once lingerie. What a pussycat. But why am I telling *you*?"

"I've enjoyed our little comic foreplay, Caine. But I don't think you appreciate the seriousness of what I'm asking you. I need answers."

"Or else what; you'll part my head with a bronze bird? I don't care if you've killed more people than cancer."

I could suddenly see a small vein in Blondie's neck. And his reply was entirely too smooth. "You misunderstand me. The people I represent had a business deal with Evert. But we didn't get to close the deal. His misfortune could be the making of yours."

"I already have a retirement program."

"You're not so funny."

"It's killin' me."

"Must we continue to play games, Professor? Look, I'll make it easy for you. Evert gave you something to hold. You thought nothing of it until he was. . .until he died. Maybe you didn't even look at it. But now your shorts are in a bunch over what to do. Well, I'm your answer. I just want to help."

"I'll try to remember you're on my side."

"So, what d'you think Professor?"

"If I could think, I'd have run out when you came in." What to do? I felt like the title of my favorite 1930s Robert Benchley humor book, *My Ten Years in a Quandary and How They Grew*.

"I'm waiting."

"The only way you'll get something out of me is to hold a bright object in front of me and twirl it."

"Okay Professor, you film-geek auteur type, you can't say I didn't give you a chance. But this isn't the end of it." With that he hopped down as if from a high perch and left the office muttering, like a spoiled child taking his ball and bat home and ending the game — as if he had not been the one responsible for finishing our conversation.

I watched his exit all the way down the hall. He never stopped rattling on to himself. The faster he mumbled the faster he walked, all the while his hands and arms were moving, like he was Leonard Bernstein's illegitimate midget son, pissed that his baton was miniature, too. I resisted the temptation to yell, "Send me a postcard from crazy town."

As luck would have it, Holly entered the hall just as our unhappy little hood was leaving it. She rolled her eyes as she passed him and suppressed a giggle (I could tell she was biting her lip, my daughter's favorite way of suppressing laughter, other than the ever popular pencil stabbing of one's leg).

"What's with the little sunshine man?" she asked as she entered my office. "And why are you watching him?"

"What happens in the game of cat and mouse, if the cat is retarded?"

Holly responded by giving me one of her patented Conan O'Brien imitations, "HUH!"

"Munchkin boy was just here paying me a rather unpleasant visit. I actually might need to lay low, something I never thought I'd hear myself say."

"I didn't think you could get any lower, Pop."

"And I hate those 'talks' you have with your mom. What I mean is, the little jerk threatened me. Said he'd given me a chance."

"What did he say!?" she asked.

"He's working for someone who thinks Evert gave me something, and he offered to 'help' me unload it."

"The plot thickens. And it's getting a little scary. Maybe we should go on the offensive and tail the little shit, bust some heads."

"Who are you, Al Capone? What's next, you growling through your teeth, 'I'm like the scratchy stuff on the side of a matchbox.'"

Laughing, she said, "No, but I like that line. So what's the plan?"

"The plan is there is no plan. We'll just have to make it up as we go."

Holly smiled and said, "I can live with that."

"I hope we *both* continue to live with that. So how about we walk over to my apartment and get a bite to eat?"

"Good call. I'm so hungry I could strip search a mouse for the last piece of cheese."

We left the building as dusk descended upon the campus. It was just a four-block walk on McIntyre Avenue, the main campus thoroughfare, over to my place. Quickly lost in conversation, we didn't initially notice the big Buick, which had pulled up as innocent as Christmas, three car lengths behind us. In fact, we expected a window to come down, with someone asking for directions. Instead, it held back, like a cast iron bull perusing its next target.

The awkward silence which surrounded this odd standoff suddenly exploded with the roar of a gunned engine, and squealing tires. The loud thud of the heavy Buick's undercarriage added to the din as the car jumped the curb and headed straight at us. Now, in the typical movie we would somehow have been able to outrun the killer car. But in bone-crushing reality, we'd just have to find another way.

I grabbed Holly's arm, and we both scrambled behind a nearby cluster of oak trees, effectively using their trunks as a shield against an auto Armageddon. But whether out-of-control, or simply leaving a murderous message, the Buick slammed into the specific tree behind which we cowered. It hit the oak with enough force to bounce Holly and me back a good ten feet. Then the car roared out of this wooded area in reverse, its spinning tires spraying dirt and chunks of campus lawn raining down everywhere. An audible switching of gears soon followed and the car accelerated away from us at a high speed.

Holly and I looked at each other in disbelief. What kind of twisted scenario had we stumbled into? I'd never advised Holly on what to do in such a situation (auto assassination comes up so seldom in father-daughter relationship books). So I was pleased that we'd both instinctively headed for the trees, instead of trying to be movie track stars and outrun the mother of all Buicks. Yet, our immediate response was much more pragmatic.

"Are you all right?" came out of both our mouths almost simultaneously. And we followed our still stunned okay nods to each other with a final bit of concurrent stereo speech, "The midget?"

Standing up and brushing each other off, Holly asked, "You wouldn't have any industrial strength Prozac, would you?"

Smiling, I added, "I'm more in the market for some adult Depends. How does that scared-to-death line go, 'First you say it, and then you do it.'"

Holly topped my attempt at humor by doing a dead-on impersonation of Sally Fields, "They hate me, they really hate me."

Laughing, I asked, "Did you get a look at the guy driving the car?"

Returning to her regular voice, she said, "No, I was too busy having a stroke. Elvis could've been driving –"

"I'm sure it wasn't Elvis. We would've noticed the reflection off the jumpsuit."

"Okay Pop, we'll take Elvis off the suspect list. Seriously, any ideas on who tried to run us down?"

"I do recognize the car now. It seems likely to involve our little friend, at some level."

"Very pun-ny, Dad. That's the shrimp I passed in the hall?"

"One and the same. And his car I recognize from Evert's funeral."

"What would he have been thinking?"

"What would he have been thinking with?"

Ignoring me, she said, "So your little tit-for-tat resulted in this?"

"It would seem so, unless we're into a Stephen King *Christine* situation, you know, where we simply have a car with demonic powers pissed off at us."

Smiling, Holly said, "That would explain our not noticing the driver. Of course, *Christine* was a Plymouth, a make with plenty to be steamed about. Buicks somehow strike me as a happier breed. . .smug and self-centered."

"As I think about it now, I don't believe whoever was behind the wheel was really out to kill us."

"Well, pardon me all to hell, Dad, but it seemed pretty convincing to me."

"Oh, I know, I was scared, too. But if someone had wanted to flatten us, they wouldn't have stopped first, and waited for us to notice them."

"Why?"

"That I don't know, but it probably means I'll be getting some more noirish company sometime soon."

"You mean like the Munchkin?"

"Or that looker at Evert's memorial service."

"Looker?"

"There was a sexy mystery woman in black — that went with the big blue car. She came in late, sat in the back. Mark nearly wet himself."

"It wouldn't take much," Holly said.

"No, this time Mark was entitled." By now we'd reached my apartment, a second story walk-up in an old brownstone. Like my office, the apartment was full of books and original framed posters. Given Evert's murder and the possible Chaplin film connection, the poster that seemed to jump out at Holly and me as we came into the apartment was a full-sheet for the post-Charlie *Monsieur Verdoux*, which screamed in blood red lettering "See a Murderous Chaplin." This was film noir meets dark comedy, with Chaplin's title character marrying a succession of wealthy widows, only to methodically knock them off.

Neither of us mentioned the poster. Holly immediately turned on the television, as was her habit upon entering any room with a small screen, and sat down with the remote. (Have you ever noticed when you're channel surfing with the remote all the programming sucks, but in the hands of someone else, every show snippet looks and/or sounds fascinating?) I was just heading to the library phone to call Mark when Holly suddenly yelled, "Get in here Dad, they're doing a news item about Evert." But it was nothing we didn't know. Going back to what Holly called "book central," I noticed my biography of Chaplin on the table by the phone. Evert had returned it to me the day before he turned up dead, and I hadn't put it back on the shelf yet. What made me now pick up the book and leaf through it I don't know — one of life's ongoingly random acts. But in the section on Chaplin's brief marriage to Mildred Harris a note card fell from the book. Startled, I picked up the paper and read in Evert's handwriting:

To be considered for your second edition: Harris was my mother! But unfortunately, Charlie was long gone by then. "Daddy" turned out to be one of Mother's later nefarious companions — Maxie "High Life" Evans, a former vaudeville dancer who disappeared shortly after I arrived. Anyway, I thought you should know.

"Holly," I shouted. "Come here! You've got to hear this!"

Chapter 4

My emotions were mixed. I felt I had been caught in a . . .
union that had no vital basis. Yet I had always wanted a
wife, and Mildred was young and pretty, not quite nine-
teen, and though I was ten years older, perhaps it would
work out all right.

—*Chaplin's autobiography*

The note from Evert had made us too antsy to stay at home. Instead, we decided to go eat in the nearby "university village," a series
of restaurant/bars and shops close to campus. As we walked Holly
said, "Give me the lowdown on Mildred Harris."

"Joe Professor, or just the *Cliff Notes* version?" I asked.

"Dazzle me," she said.

"You're asking for it," I answered. "I did a lecture on her last year
for a Chaplin symposium." But before I could start I was distracted
by Holly's sudden need to keep looking behind us. "What's with all
this turning around?" I asked.

"Sorry, I just don't want that Buick to sneak up on us again. But
go on," she said.

"Okay, Harris was a sexy young actress with whom Chaplin became infatuated. Mildred soon announced she was pregnant, and they
were married almost immediately. But her condition proved to be, as
Chaplin later so diplomatically put it, a "false alarm.""

"Wasn't he pissed at being suckered?" asked Holly.

"Hold that thought," I said. We had reached our favorite village
eatery, a place called the McIntyre Street Bar and Grill. Getting a
booth by the window, a college age waitress came over with menus.
She had shockingly red hair, like the title character in *Run Lola Run*,

and enough body piercings to change the local electromagnetic field. Taking a cue from her T-shirt, which proclaimed — "Pabst Beer, Helping the Ugly Have Sex Since 1892," I ordered a beer, and underage Holly went with a soft drink. After we put in our food requests, I answered Holly's question. "The Chaplin biography film, with Robert Downey, Jr., plays him pissed. But in reality it wasn't that simple."

"It seldom is," Holly added softly.

"Chaplin and Harris stuck it out for a while, and she actually became pregnant," I said.

"They had a baby?" asked Holly in wide-eyed amazement.

"Yeah, but he was malformed, and only lived three days. His grave stone simply said, 'The Little Mouse,' their pet name for him.

"How sad," said Holly, her eyes suddenly watery.

"Anyway, the marriage lasted two years, and she got a fat divorce settlement — which was soon spent. Then it was back to periodic films —"

"Anything I would have seen?" Holly inquired.

"The only picture that gets any regular TV air time is a Three Stooges short from the 1930s called *Movie Maniacs*. Mildred plays a film star, not without appeal. Had enough?"

"I want more than enough."

At this point, two former students briefly stopped to say "hi" on their way out. This was one of the ongoing perks of being a professor, except when they wanted to borrow money.

The split second they were gone the mystery-obsessed Holly fired another question. "Where does Evert fit in here?"

"Well, despite our informative note card take on 'High Life' Evans, I don't think Evert really knew who his father was, because Mildred had at least two other short marriages after Chaplin. Poor shmuck, it was probably just easier to keep his mother's name. But why he would have kept Momsie's identity quiet, I don't know. However, it certainly helps explain Evert's interest in Chaplin and silent film."

"Whatever became of Mildred?" asked Holly.

"More sad stuff," I said. "Alcoholism, bouts of depression, fallen arches, the whole nine yards."

Laughing, Holly said, "Seriously, what happened to Mildred?"

"Actually, drinking and depression were problems for her. But I've never gotten a straight answer about the arches. She died after surgery, sometime in the 1940s."

Genuinely interested, Holly asked, "How old was she?"

"Just in her early forties," I answered.

Once again moved, Holly asked, "Did Evert ever say anything about his mother?"

"Maybe once, in passing, that she had a nice singing voice. At the time, I was thinking in terms of goodnight lullabies. But in later years, Mildred had a mildly successful cabaret act, both in vaudeville and nightclubs."

The food arrived at this point, and we took a short break from the world of Mildred Harris. As our waitress disappeared Holly and I did our standard naval salute in her direction, acknowledging the special status of this café society sorcerer who brings us what we request.

As the meal wound down I could see Holly getting that "let's get back to our mystery look." She asked, "Do you think Evert had any later contact with Chaplin, maybe through his mother?"

"Your guess is as good as mine," I said.

"Actually not, you've got all those letters behind your name."

"Why, thank you, Sweetie."

"I always try to leave the crowd happy," Holly said.

"Is that our cue to leave?" I ask.

"Yeah, if you don't mind. I know it's early, but it's been a long day. I damn near pulled an all-nighter last night studying for a lit exam. And then there was our little adventure with the Buick."

Walking Holly back to her dorm I asked her about the exam.

"I like words but I'm not crazy about complete sentences," she said.

"Boy, you are burned out, Kiddo."

Smiling, she nodded and said, "If I don't get some sleep I'm going to look like Keith Richards."

"Hang in there, we're almost to your dorm. You know, when I was your age I was going to be the next Hemingway. But I couldn't make the weight."

Laughing while patting my stomach she said, "I don't know, I think you're coming right along with the weight, Pop."

After safely depositing Holly at her dorm I walked back to my apartment. Maybe Holly's anxiety had rubbed off on me, because I found myself looking behind me every six paces. Thankfully, I was always alone. At the apartment I turned on all the lights, but I resisted a temptation to check under my bed.

Holly called to make sure I was home safe, then it was writing time, *the* special part of the day. I work at a flat oak library table where a Tiffany Lamp gives out the warmest gold light. Like most writers, I have what novelist Michael Chabon calls the "midnight disease," the need to scribble into the wee hours. It's quiet, and the problems of the day seem to fall away, unless they involve murder close to home, and a near-miss showdown with a Buick. Still, writing was my lifeline to sanity. As one of my college professors used to say, "Writing is not life, but I think that sometimes it can be a way back to life."

Of course, it's valued differently around the world. Geoffrey Cotterell said, "In America only the successful writer is important, in France all writers are important, in England no writer is important, in Australia you have to explain what a writer is."

My first wife, Holly's mother, had once complained she could never compete with my mistress — writing. I'd long been fascinated with how the process of creating a book was like falling in love — the newness, the excitement of filtering the world through a fresh relationship — literally reinventing yourself. But as an army of authors have stated about love, "Art is where you get it right." That is, while one is often fated to eventually suffer a relationship train wreck (notwithstanding the initial fun), you can only guarantee yourself a great partner if you're writing both parts. And in that case it becomes as simple and straight-forward as the alphabet — with just as many possibilities.

I knocked off at three. At least that was when I stretched out on a nearby couch. My pattern is to work until I'm overcome by exhaustion. Someday they'll probably find me impaled on my pencil. Anyway, I was awakened by the phone at eight. At least I think it was eight. My eyes don't focus well until early afternoon. It was Holly.

"Hello, Sleepy Head. Did you crash on the couch again?" she asked.

"It's convenient," I said.

"You might as well sublet your bedroom. Hey, just as a lark, you could tuck in early sometime and actually get in eight hours."

"I get by okay," I said.

"What exactly does 'get by' mean?" she asked. "I can 'get by' with little sleep, too. If 'get by' means drooling, or watching reruns of *Gilligan's Island*. Pop, some mornings you look like someone they forgot to bury."

"No, I just wasn't there when they came around . . . . When I was a kid your Uncle Wally called sleep 'death's younger brother.' I've been a reluctant sleeper ever since."

"Funny. But did Wally really say that, or are you getting colorful with your bio again?"

"Well, as the storyteller once said, 'It might not have happened exactly that way, but that's how I remember it.'"

"If you slept more, you'd dream more — which is ideal, because you'd meet a better class of people," said Holly. "Oh, before I forget, I got an appointment for us with Mrs. Franklin first thing tomorrow."

"Thanks. Let's hope we can figure out something about Evert's key."

"Do you mind if I drop over in a little bit?" asked Holly. "I need to check out your books on comedy theory."

"Sure, no problem." Still suffering through my normal morning malaise, I then stumbled into the bathroom and did my standard Bob Fosse *All That Jazz* shower sequence — the prolonged soak that eventually revives the victim, though I seldom repeat that picture's post-shower mantra, "It's show time." I shaved and put on my film professor uniform — jeans, a blue work shirt, and a brown corduroy jacket. But there were no leather patches on the elbows. I only carry my academic clichés so far. A little before nine I was opening my door to Holly, all dolled up in her favorite Led Zeppelin T-shirt, jeans, and a New York Yankee/Derek Jeter windbreaker. She presented me with my morning newspaper, retrieved from the stoop.

"Care for some breakfast?" I asked, as she swept past me.

"Count me in," she said. And we were soon downing bagels and cream cheese, while reading the paper.

"Hey, here's something about Evert," I said.

"What does it say?" Holly asked.

"Give me a minute." I then proceeded to speed read the front page article.

"Well?" said an impatient Holly.

"It looks like a rehash of last night's news byte. But here's a new wrinkle — when Evert's mother died they were estranged."

"Does it say why?" Holly asked. But before I could read on she was peppering the airways with, "Shit, shit, shit!" She had managed to drop her second bagel half on the floor, cream cheese side down. "Did you see that landing?" she asked. "I'm sure the Romanian judge would have given me a 10."

"Don't worry about it," I said. Handing her the front page, I cleaned up the crash site and began toasting her another bagel. As I did this Holly read the Evert article. By the time her bagel was ready I noticed almost a scowl on her brow. "Did I miss something?" I asked.

"It appears Evert was also at odds with a stepsister," she answered.

"I guess I missed that," I said.

"Well, it's near the end of the piece."

As I toasted another bagel for myself I asked, "How do they work the stepsister in?"

"When Harris died, the children battled over whatever modest possessions constituted her estate. The stepsister, one Jessica Harris, claimed at the time, and I quote, 'Evert was always withdrawn. He never thought about what was best for Mother.'"

Holly then seemed to accentuate those tough words by taking a crunchy bite of her bagel. We finished eating without any further talk, and then I volunteered, "If things were somewhat strained between Mildred and Evert, I'm betting it was because vaudeville and nightclubs kept her on the road. Touring during the Depression wouldn't have left much time for being a parent."

We talked about Evert a few more minutes and then she headed off to class, while I glanced over my lecture notes for my own first class of the day. An hour later, as I walked down the film department's inner hallway towards my office, I was startled to see my door ajar. Quickening my pace, I looked in on a depressing sight.

Someone had ransacked my office. There's nothing like starting the day with a little personal violation. On the plus side, however, it was not the traditional movie-style ransacking, where everything is trashed. You know, the kind of scene Bogie is always coming in on. Instead, most of my violated stuff (file folders, books, film magazines, and lecture notebooks) were neatly stacked on the floor around my office, like it was moving day back in the old neighborhood.

My first thought, of course, was Evert's mystery poster. So, like a hungry man going after a waffle, I closed my door and checked the hiding place behind the framed one-sheet poster of Chaplin's *Modern Times*. Praise Jesus, it was still there. I must confess to mixed feelings about this — happy I still had it, yet almost wishing it were gone. What had Evert gotten me into?

Looking around my office at all the various tidy stacks, however, I had to chuckle — a fastidious intruder, what would they think of next? Robin Williams has a line about gay intruders, who had a tendency to break into homes and redecorate them. . .makeovers which always included countless pictures of Joan Crawford and Judy Garland.

Before I could start putting the place back together, or belt out some show tunes, there was a knock on the door. I opened up the door and it was Dr. Charles, the head of the department. He stared at my politely ransacked office and gave me a look like I'd smacked him with a sock full of nickels.

"Are you leaving us?" he asked, only half kidding.

"No, just making room for the new hot tub and wet bar," I said.

Charles was a great chair. He kept the department running smoothly without getting in the way of each prof's personal academic area. We also played tennis on a regular basis, though I was not in his league. He could fall out of bed on Christmas morning and still serve an ace. He was a great middle-aged athlete in spite of the fact that he smoked two packs a day. For him, tobacco was one of the basic food groups. Indeed, he was on his way outdoors for a puff when he got curious about my closed door and gave it a knock.

"Ha, ha, David," he said. "Seriously, what gives with everything on the floor?"

"Well Chief, I hate to jump to conclusions but it appears that my office has been searched."

"You're kidding. What would anyone be looking for? What have you gotten mixed up in?" he asked.

Playing dumb, I said, "I haven't a clue. What with taking care of my paper route, choir practice, and my volunteer work at the orphanage, I don't always stay on top of things."

"Is anything missing?" he asked.

"I don't know. I really haven't had time to inventory things. But my few humble valuables on the walls are still with me."

Charles cluck-clucked a little more, then said he was going to have to call security. So when I returned from teaching my class — an hour and a half later — a campus cop was waiting for me, Officer Roberts. He looked like a cross between actor Nathan Lane and a Flintstone vitamin. Consistent with this goofy, pleasantly ugly appearance, he asked, "What's going on here? First murder, and now this."

"You got me," I said.

Roberts then proceeded to ask the litany of officialdom questions, such as who I was, what I did, and so on. After that promising beginning, he had gone humorless on me, as if he'd had a charisma bypass. Then he threw a surprise question my way, "Were you close to Evert Harris?"

Up until this point Roberts had seemed to be operating at the intellectual level of moss. But maybe that was part of his plan, playing what is referred to in literary circles as the "wise fool." Caught off guard for an answer, I mumbled, "No more than anyone in the department."

"Do you think this [he gestured around my office] had anything to do with the murder victim?" he asked.

Obviously, this was a scary idea — a scary idea which had been running through my head since the adventure with the Buick. For once I gave Roberts an honest reaction, "It's possible but I wouldn't know where to begin. Am I in danger?

"Oh, I don't think so. This could've just been a student prank over grades." But his reading of these lines was not too convincing.

"When can I start putting my office back together?" I asked.

"Anytime. I've already had someone from my office take photos while you were in class. And I think I've got all the notes I need." Reaching out to shake my hand he added, "Take care of yourself, Professor Caine."

Surprised but appreciative of the apparent concern, I thanked him, and was soon alone with my pick-up chores. But not for long. Just as I was thinking I should share Evert's mystery game with the police, Holly nosed into the room like bumbling Inspector Clouseau looking for clues. Checking out the systematically disheveled office she dryly observed, "Maid's day to dust?"

"No, but between a ransacked office and our adventure with that Buick, it's time to talk. As much as I enjoy blowing a playful raspberry at bad guys, my fascination with all things Chaplin has put you at risk. I'm a shitty dad —"

"You're not a shitty dad," she said, in a much calmer voice than my flirting with stress tone. "Besides, even if we go to the cops, who's to say midget man and company still wouldn't come after us? Evert died to have this lost film shown. If we stop now, maybe we're safe but the Charlie picture is lost forever. 'You'll regret it. Maybe not today, and maybe not tomorrow, but soon and for the rest of your life—'."

"Not *Casablanca*."

"Hey, I don't apologize. It was a natural segue and I took it."

"'Here's looking at you, kid.'"

"Puns are worse, Dad. But getting back to our personal film noir, we don't have enough facts yet to help out the cops, or anyone else. I mean, you could chart our progress with a sun dial. Let's just let it ride for now."

Thank goodness for Holly and her Seinfeld-sprinkled-with-acid personality. The detective duo of Caine and Caine remained on the case. We worked several hours putting the place back together, assisted by the fact that we were waiting out a top-notch rain storm which had come up — a regular "frog strangler," to borrow a phrase from Andy Griffith. But even before the rain hit I remember thinking what a fitting metaphor, the gathering storm, for this Evert/Chaplin mystery.

Chapter 5

Without question, marriage [to Mildred] was having a [negative] effect on my creative faculties. After [the film] Sunnyside I was at my wit's end for an idea.
—*Chaplin's autobiography*

Holly and I met Mrs. Franklin the following morning at my daughter's old high school. Early. Thank you, Holly. Anyway, I knew I was going to like Betty Franklin as soon as we stepped into her office. Book city. She reminded me of my great grandmother — large brown eyes and tightly braided silver gray hair wrapped closely to her head. She had on a brown peasant blouse and a long skirt.

"Holly, so good to see you," said Mrs. Franklin, as she hugged my daughter. And then reaching a hand out to me added, "Dr. Caine, this is an honor. Indeed, I have a favor to ask." With that she started to sort through a stack of papers and journals on her desk that reminded me of W. C. Fields' roll top disarray in *The Man on the Flying Trapeze*. Soon Mrs. Franklin had fished a book out and thrust it towards me. "Would you be so good as to sign this for me?" Fittingly, it was a paperback I'd done on Groucho Marx and W. C. Fields entitled *Huckster Comedians.*

"I'm flattered," I said, as I took the book from her. I opened it to the title page for an autograph and a short note — "Some people think I'm self-absorbed, but if you just knew me better."

As I wrote she observed, "I especially enjoyed your suggestion on how Groucho might respond to the Middle East today — 'War over religion is like killing someone over who has better imaginary friends.'"

Taking the book back she paused to read my inscription, chuckled, and then said, "Oh, thank you so much! Now [motioning us to sit down]. How can *I* help *you*? You sounded a little mysterious on the phone."

Pulling Evert's key out of my pocket I handed it to Mrs. Franklin and said, "Holly thought you might be able to tell us something about this key."

Putting on her glasses, which hung from a ribbon around her neck, she only briefly examined the key and said, "Why, yes. I think maybe I can." With that, she smiled and pointed towards a framed object on the opposite wall. As I turned to better see the item I noticed that Holly was already staring at it — transfixed. A twin key to the one I'd just handed her was the framed object of all this attention.

"These keys are certainly a blast from the past. I used to wear mine on a chain as antique jewelry. That's what you remember seeing, isn't it, Holly?"

"It was hard to forget," said Holly. "You were famous for it."

"How nicely you put that, dear! I'm well aware that the students all thought I was an antique myself. Every school year there was a variation of 'Who really discovered electricity — you or your husband Ben?' or 'Love the key. Where's the kite?'"

Sheepishly, Holly said, "We only teased the teachers we loved."

"Well," I said, "Holly hadn't given me all this background info, Mrs. Franklin. I just hope that lightning will strike twice and you can help us discover the answer to this key business."

"Ugh," said Mrs. Franklin, "another groaner I've heard before. But yes, back to the keys. Long before you came, our university's original four buildings — one of which has become the lab school where I teach, and one which has become the home of your department offices — each had a built-in wall safe in its main office. Over the years, as the buildings' uses were changed and many remodelings took place, the use for these safes fell by the wayside.

"How did you become keeper of the key?" Holly asked.

"Early in my tenure, when Moses was a boy, I was put in charge of the 'hideaway.' That's what they called it then, the 'hideaway.' Anyway, even then, there wasn't much in it. I'd admired the key one day in the office and the next thing you know, Mr. Simpson, the principal then, made it my responsibility."

"Was it still being used when you wore the key around your neck, back when I was in high school?" asked Holly.

"Oh my no, dear. Even then, it was a thing of the past," Mrs. Franklin said.

"Any thoughts on the 'hideaway' status in my building?" I asked.

"It's anyone's guess where it would be now," said Mrs. Franklin.

"How do you mean?" Holly asked.

"The North Quad, as we used to call it, has been made over more times than my Aunt Maude," said Mrs. Franklin. "Before the film department, the Quad was home to sociology, and before that history . . . ."

"Just between you and me and a fence post, I've got reason to believe a 'hideaway' still exists in the Quad."

"Yes, of course, the key," she said. And with that she picked up Evert's key from her desk and looked at it as intently as one would a magic wand. Then, almost reluctantly, she handed it back to me.

"Mrs. Franklin, this is probably all just a shot in the dark. And keep in mind, you're talking to someone who probably couldn't track buffaloes in the snow. But if you were going to give a poor novice sleuth a tip on finding the North Quad 'hideaway," what would it be?" I asked.

Chuckling, she affectionately observed, "You're just going to have to look, Sonny."

Holly laughed out loud, and I said, "Well, anytime you need a straight man . . . ."

After a pause, Mrs. Franklin ventured, "I don't know if this would help but the opening for the 'hideaway' in this building was actually behind some decorative wood trim. Plus, the old offices were huge. Remodeling often resulted in sizing them down —"

"So this 'hideaway' might be in a newer adjoining room?" I asked.

"That would be my bet," she said.

"Well, Mrs. Franklin, you've really been helpful. If Holly and I crack this, it'll be thanks to you."

As we got up to leave, she again hugged Holly and said, "Don't be a stranger." Turning to me she added, "Good luck with your treasure hunt."

"Thanks," I replied. "Not to sound melodramatic, or anything, but if anyone asks, we never had this conversation."

"What conversation?" she said.

That night Holly and I paid an after hours visit to my department's main office. As with all full-time faculty, I had both a key to the building, and the office. As an occasional late night visitor to the building, usually with regard to my writing, I knew the custodial staff should not be on duty. My only concern was we'd run into another nocturnal professor. But that couldn't be helped. Holly was jumpy that the midget in yellow would surface. These worries notwithstanding, we seemed to have every advantage, including a university lighting policy that had the fluorescent lamps burning around the clock. This disappointed Holly, who wanted to stalk about with a flashlight.

Like fugitives from a Three Stooges detective movie, we tapped and pressed against every square inch of the main office wall space, but with no luck. Holly bumped into a floor lamp at one point and ad-libbed in a stage whisper, "I didn't know the lights were against me."

I snorted, and then whispered back to her, "Waddya think, should we try Evert's office?"

"Can you get us in?"

"Yeah, I think so. Linda, the secretary, keeps the department's master key under her desk blotter."

"You're kidding."

"No, we've got quite the security system here," I said.

We were soon in Evert's office, the crime scene tape having been removed the previous day. It looked like he'd just stepped out for a smoke. Fittingly, there were several Chaplin books stacked on his desk. Scary. Somehow I'd assumed his stuff would have been packed up and gone.

"Do you think the 'hideaway' is in here?" Holly asked.

"We can hope. But we weren't getting anywhere out there," I said.

"It does make sense," Holly added, "that Evert might have found the 'hideaway' if it were right under his nose."

"And Evert's office is the closest to the main office, if Mrs. Franklin's theory on this once all being one room has any credence," I said.

Holly and I then proceeded to go into our tapping and pressing routine. The casual observer might have mistaken us for termite inspectors, or possibly Helen Keller clones in search of Braille wall graffiti. Just when it seemed that we had struck out on our minor league breaking-and-entering caper, Holly suggested we move Evert's desk away from the wall. Now, we'd already moved a few things, from an end table and chairs, to a small book shelf. But the desk would represent a mother of a move. Where's that forklift when you need it?

Unlike the traditional university issue flat metal desk, Evert had a large wooden roll top, which blocked a goodly portion of the wall. To simplify our task, we removed all the drawers before making like Arnold Schwarzenegger. After much straining and many whispered obscenities, we had the desk away from the wall. (Getting a hernia was not something I remembered reading about in your basic "How to be a detective" literature.)

Once the roll top was out, two small ridges in the wall were apparent — ridges that easily could have supported decorative wood trim. And a closer examination of the space revealed a painted-over latched door roughly eight by ten inches in size. But there was no apparent lock or triggering mechanism.

This proved a poser but then Holly noted that the paint alongside a nearby plug-in was scuffed. Upon applying pressure in that direction, the plastic plug-in cover swiveled aside, revealing a small lock.

Evert's key was a perfect fit, and presto, the spring activated door of the 'hideaway' popped open. Holly squealed and I pumped my fist — we were in business. At this point, some people might have considered turning over our discoveries to the police. But Holly and I were now so caught up in Evert's game that the subject never surfaced.

Inside the safe-like opening was a wooden box with a hinged top, slightly larger than a cigar box. It contained several old newspaper and magazine clippings brittle with age. Indeed, the bottom of the box had a layer of the chaff-like particles from the self-destructing discolored pulp paper. The box also had two letters with postdates from the 1920s, and one addressed to Chaplin but apparently never sent. As much as we wanted to immediately read these documents — and Holly was practically sitting on my shoulder in order to not miss a thing — I thought it best to first return Evert's office to normal, and then retreat to my apartment. I didn't want to leave any footnotes to our visit. Moving the desk back provided one final bit of comic stress. First, we couldn't seem to budge it. Then we overcompensated and practically drove it through the wall, creating a noise we were sure had been heard in neighboring states. Laurel and Hardy would have been proud.

Like the very thieves in the night that we were, we quickly put the rest of Evert's office back together, including the drawers, and locked the door. The master key was returned to Linda's casual hiding place; and then we fairly flew back to my digs, ever so anxious to examine our findings. We looked behind us a mere six million times on the short walk, but no one seemed to follow us. Our undercover operation had been, as Dan Aykroyd used to say on *Saturday Night Live* — "Just that easy." But before Holly and I started to sell decoder rings over the internet, we now had to figure out what we'd found.

Sitting down at the kitchen table, Holly pulled the adjustable overhead lamp down close, to better enable us to check out our treasure. I carefully took the first item out of the box — a 1937 newspaper article from the *Brooklyn Daily Eagle* entitled — "First Wife of Chaplin Starts Comeback Here." Much of the brittle paper had broken away. But a section underlined in red towards the end remained intact. Holly and I read through the material, in which Mildred Harris discussed her 11-year-old son (Evert) back in California:

He's crazy about airplanes, and I don't think he'll ever go on the stage. That's funny, isn't it? I'd like to see him Christmas Day, but I'll be in Boston, of course. I hope he knows I love him.

The second item in Evert's box was an article even more fragmented with age. It was taken from a 1919 *Photoplay*, a movie fan magazine of yesteryear. Most of the pages were past salvaging, except for one criss-crossed with formerly clear tape now brown with age. Seemingly about the marriage of Chaplin and Harris, this special page had a quote by the comedian that was faintly circled in pencil: "If you could take my word for it, my bride is the sweetest, cutest, dandiest, little playmate you could find in 48 states, and quite the actress."

"Pop, that's like nothing I've ever heard credited to Chaplin."

"Evert's sad legacy, I guess. Clippings from an absentee mother, chronicling both Mildred's glory days with Chaplin, and love for her son."

"Who do you think did the underlining and circling?" Holly asked.

"I don't know as it makes any difference. The main thing is that Evert kept them all these years. It's hardly the action of someone who disliked his mother."

"How do you mean?"

"That recent Evert piece in our paper had his stepsister suggesting he was at odds with Mildred," I said. "Remember?"

"Oh, yeah. Now I do. What else is in here?" Holly asked.

I carefully picked up several more newspaper clippings, all in equally brittle brown condition. There were no highlighted portions, however, and the fragments that did survive suggested a sad desperation by Mildred merely to be remembered. A *New York Morning Telegraph* article from 1926 was entitled, "Chaplin's Blonde Ex-Wife, Once A Star, Only A Brunette Extra Now." And a *New York Sun* profile from ten years later had the small headline, "First Wife of Chaplin Tries Burlesque." Ironically, her act involved singing the song, "Where Are You?" and then doing an impersonation of an actress famous for wanting to be left alone, Greta Garbo. Obviously, being left alone was the last thing on Mildred Harris' mind.

"I wonder if Harris ever thought about the fact that when she was a Hollywood star, Garbo was just a rinse girl working in a Stockholm beauty parlor?" I ventured.

"Probably every waking moment," said Holly.

Given the Chaplin-Christ connection driving our treasure hunt, a final article item from the box, an undated partial page from the silent film publication *Motion Picture Magazine*, was especially diverting. An interviewer was asking the comedian for his thoughts on Jesus. Chaplin observed, "Christ was evidently a man of the utmost social charm, with humor. You read of Him in the Bible as a dinner guest at the houses of the rich and poor — and an honored guest. He was what we call a mixer, yet He was always alone. He tried to give His message to the world, and nobody understood Him. That is the supreme tragedy." But sadly, that was all that remained of the piece. Still, it was a revealing window to Chaplin's thoughts — Christ as a humorous "mixer."

In the days to come we would more carefully pore over every journalistic scrap of paper, with such intensity that I was afraid we would absorb the ink right off the page. But now we were more anxious to read the letters at the bottom of Evert's box.

The first was still in its original powder blue envelope. Though addressed to Chaplin, it had apparently never been sent. The envelope's two-cent George Washington stamp had not been cancelled, nor had the backside flap been sealed. Removing the letter, which was written in a flowery hand upon matching powder blue stationery, I took a deep breath and began to read:

Dearest Charlie,

I loved you as much as it's possible for me to love any man. At the time of the divorce Mother asked me if you still loved me. I told her I didn't know, and I didn't think you knew. But we were together long enough for me to know you loved me for a time. And I am sure you have never forgotten that. So I am not as surprised as you might think about this kind offer to play Mary in your next picture. Hope is a frail ally, but an ally none-the-less. I don't want this chance for money, or fame, I want it as a souvenir of us. I cannot wait for your return from England.

As Always, Mildred

"Is it dated?" asked Holly

"No," I answered. "But it has to have been sometime in 1921. It fits the time schedule we constructed after I got the *Time Machine* poster."

"Can you believe this?" said Holly, as excited as a child at Christmas. "Who's next?" she asked.

Reaching carefully into our treasure box, I fished out a letter to Evert, sans envelope, dated July 30, 1944, and read:

I was so sorry about your mother's passing. She was no saint but she wasn't really a bad kid, and Charlie, God bless him, loused her up good. At first, Mildred maybe saw him as a ticket to the high life in movies. But I know that once she climbed on board she tried to be a good wife, and he ended up treating her like she was dirt.

I think casting Mildred in his Christ picture was Charlie's way of saying he was sorry. But the whole being sorry thing was a tough road to hoe for him. Oh, it wasn't like he had to go to Oz to get a heart. Charlie could be very sentimental. Yet his mercurial mood changes kept the sorry quotient to a minimum. Then he closed up shop on the movie, and made like it never happened. It might have been Mildred's ticket. We'll never know.

I best close. This has gone beyond a letter, to a regular visit. I always counted Mildred as a close friend. Hopefully, we can maintain a friendship, too.

Love, Marion

This time I was the one as thrilled as a child opening presents. But before I could do a cartwheel, a totally absorbed Holly said, "Is this Marion D-A-V-I-E-S, as in the mistress of William Randolph Hearst?!"

"One and the same. "I'm glad our trip to Hearst's castle was not lost on you." We'd visited the media magnate's California palace two summers before.

"Well, that and the fact you've made me watch *Citizen Kane* a million times," she said. [Hearst was the inspiration for this Orson Welles' film classic.]

"Let it go half-pint; let it go."

"Do me a favor, Pop —"

"Does it involve a donkey?"

"You're a sick man, Dad. All I wanted was some romantic background on Charlie and Marion. It seems like I remember you telling me they were once a couple."

"Never officially. Marion was not about to give up her Hearst gravy train. But Charlie and Marion were said to have had an affair which so enraged W. R., as she called Hearst, that he tried to kill Chaplin."

"What happened?" asked Holly.

"Well, there are conflicting stories but both involve the death of prominent film producer, Thomas Ince, on Hearst's yacht — later referred to as 'Hearst's Hearse.'"

"Go on," said Holly.

"One account has Hearst catching Charlie and Marion in the act, and in the ensuing chase, W. R. accidentally gunned down Ince."

"And the other story?" asked Holly.

"This one has less of a Keystone Kop flavor to it. Ince was said to resemble Charlie in build and coloring. Hearst, already suspicious of Chaplin, caught Marion and Ince in a compromising situation. Assuming it was Charlie, W. R. shot and killed Ince."

"How did he get away with it?" asked Holly.

"How does anyone get away with anything? Money, power. . . Hearst was just this side of deity. People joked that he once double-dated with God. The guests on 'Hearst's Hearse' were given a 'deal they couldn't refuse.'" Plus, cover-ups don't have to be that complex. Churchill once said, 'The best vote against democracy is to spend five minutes with the average voter.'"

"And where does this leave us in our search for *Charlie and the Time Machine*?"

"Well, with both Mildred and Marion discussing the picture, it must have been made, or at least started. We couldn't be sure of that when all we had was Evert's poster."

"Speaking of which, are there any more letters in the box?" asked Holly.

"One, I believe." And I carefully drew out another piece of correspondence. This envelope-less letter, dated 1928, was on parchment-like stationery:

Dear Mildred, I'm afraid I'm one of those cases where the juice ain't worth the squeeze. I don't really have any influence with Charlie anymore, not that I ever had very much. But if he doesn't want to release this Jesus movie, there's really very little anyone can do.

You're the last person I expected to ever receive a letter from. As you no doubt know, I was romantically involved with Charlie, before your surprise wedding. And Charlie and I'd made over two dozen pictures together when I found out about your ceremony — in the newspaper.

At the time I was stunned, like a lost ball in high weeds. I didn't think very kind thoughts towards you for quite some time.

A "lump" came in my throat that I thought would never leave. I kept thinking of the conclusion to *The Immigrant*, where Charlie borrows two dollars for a marriage license, and then carries me over the threshold of the license bureau. Poor fellow, he had to keep reminding me that my character was a coy protesting girl. But protesting was the last thing on my mind. For once I didn't mind his tendency to do countless takes. I finally let the bad feelings go after remembering something Charlie used to say, "The more you stir an old turd, the more it stinks."

You've probably forgotten that he kept a movie of mine from seeing the light of day, too. Charlie sponsored a graduation picture of sorts for me called *Sea Gulls*, which was directed by Joseph von Sternberg.

Charlie's explanation for not releasing the movie, which was also briefly called *A Woman of the Sea*, was that Joe, whom Charlie had known in Brooklyn before his "von" days, had shot beautiful images but with an incomprehensible story.

I wish I had better news for you. But my advice would be don't rock the boat. Charlie is death on the disloyal.

Sorry to have rambled on so. What's the old vaudeville line about the longwinded type, "She must have been vaccinated with a phonograph record." That's me.

Best wishes, Edna

"What am I trying to remember about Edna Purviance?" asked Holly, as I finished reading the letter out loud. "It was Purviance, right?"

"She was an early Chaplin leading lady and onetime mistress," I said. "Even after the comedian's marriage to Mildred, Edna remained his leading lady for three, or four more years. Plus, he kept her on the payroll for the rest of her life — sort of a case of twisted chivalry."

"What's the story on *Sea Gulls*?"

"Well, Edna pretty much nails it. Chaplin was impressed with this young director, years before von Sternberg created the Marlene Dietrich phenomenon. Wanting to give Edna's solo career another jump start, after his own *A Woman of Paris* did nothing for her, Chaplin acted as a patron on a von Sternberg-Purviance picture."

Holly interrupted at this point, "Was Edna right on why the film wasn't released?"

"Probably," I said. But other explanations have surfaced on occasion, too, from Chaplin being jealous of what von Sternberg had accomplished, which seems unlikely, to the comedian being upset over the quality of Edna's performance."

"How so?" asked Holly.

"The loss of Chaplin as a lover was hard on Edna, and when he basically stopped using her as a performer she developed a drinking problem. As a sidebar, Mildred's later alcoholism was also blamed on the comedian. Anyway, when the insecure Edna was sober she sometimes suffered from mild shaking attacks, and this was what von Sternberg would have had to work around. But lots of actors have had similar problems — like Clark Gable late in his career — and directors have been able to mask it."

"Did Joseph von ever have any public thoughts on the project?" asked Holly.

"Yeah, he did an entertainingly off-the-wall memoir called *Fun in a Chinese Laundry*, in which he diplomatically implied it was just one of Chaplin's whims."

"So, do we chalk this up as more evidence that the comedian both made and probably salted away our movie, *Charlie Chaplin and the Time Machine*?" asked Holly.

"Definitely, Edna's whole letter could be subtitled: 'Charlie kept a film of mine, too.' The only thing that bothers me is that eventually Chaplin had *Sea Gulls* destroyed," I said.

"No shit."

"But on the plus side, I don't think Evert would be leading us on this merry mystery if he didn't have a big pay-off," I said, before adding, "I hope, I hope. Otherwise this could be like the Irish cargo ship carrying yoyos . . . . It sank 44 times."

Ignoring me through a smile, Holly peered into the box and said, "That would appear to be it for our little time capsule, except for these newspaper fragments. Would you mind if I fish them out and see if I can reconstruct an article or two?"

"Be my guest but take it easy. Pour the contents out on some paper, and I'll get you a pair of tweezers to work with," I suggested. Leaving the room to get "the pinchers," as my mom called them, Holly's squeal immediately brought me back into the room. "What's the matter?" I asked.

"Pop, look what I've found!"

Chapter 6

A Charlie Chaplin *Tijuana Bible*

Evert's wooden box had a false bottom. When removed, it revealed a shallow hiding place containing a small manila envelope.
Nervously, and with Holly close by, I pulled two items from the envelope. First was a folded piece of stationery, which seemed brilliantly
white in contrast to all the discolored and brittle newsprint we'd gone
through. The longhand letter was from Evert:

Congratulations. I'm posthumously glad to see that you are the
bright fellow I thought you were. Leo McCarey always said direct-
ing was 90% casting. Anyway, by now you're probably wondering
why I didn't do something with this bombshell. After all, I am —
was — an endowed chair in silent film. This could have been the
capstone to my career. Unfortunately, as you will eventually see,
this film was a bit too personal for me. Erotic movies with one's
mother don't play well with my generation. But it's an important
picture which needs to be in our culture, and you're the unbiased
scholar to champion it. Ironically, I've always been an academic
star for whom success came easy and life came hard. And here's
life derailing what would have been my greatest success. However, as a consolation prize, I'm allowing myself the fun of spinning a mystery. And you know how much I love a good mystery.
So, in the spirit of what I've revealed about my mother, I have enclosed some carnal copy among the potential clues in this box.
Happy hunting.

—Evert

Holly let out a low whistle. "Well, father of mine, our lost movie just got dirty?"

"That's what the man said. But at the moment I'm more interested in the kinky stuff he said was in the box."

The other item from the envelope, which had been hidden in the box's false bottom, was a small paper booklet, roughly six inches wide, and four inches high. The cover page, entitled *Charlie Chaplin's Harem*, was of cheap pulp paper now brown with age. When I turned to the first page I couldn't suppress a major laugh. Giving it a quick flip-through, my laughter continued.

A startled Holly gave me the most quizzical of looks, as if to say, "Has this mystery stuff put you off your nut?" But to her credit she simply came closer and looked at the pages as I went through them. First her eyes got very big, and then she stammered, "They're, they're dirty comics of Charlie."

"Right you are, dear. It's what used to be called a *Tijuana Bible*. This is from back in the good old days, when air and water were clean, and sex was dirty. But if you were looking for the entertainment equivalent of a good, plain homecooked meal, this was not the ticket. What we have here is essentially *Naked Lunch*."

"Come again?" Holly asked, still struggling with the concept of a *Tijuana Bible*.

"During the 1920s and 30s these were a popular form of underground comic book art." I began, "Dad said —"

"Did I miss a meeting? Grandpa had these?" asked an incredulous Holly.

"Sure. They were fairly common. Anyway, he said they were also called *Eight Pagers*, the standard length. They pretty much speak for themselves, or don't speak for themselves, depending on your frame of mind."

With a bemused shake of her head, Holly asked, "And just how does this tie in with our mystery?"

"I don't know. Let's check it out and see." Laying *Charlie Chaplin's Harem* on the table, we carefully went through the brittle-with-age booklet. There was one pornographically drawn comic panel per page, with the flip side of each page being blank. And there were eight pages.

The black and white drawings were not quite the funny papers, though the pictorial layouts were a bit more ambitious — if you know what I mean. And while Holly was a grown woman, I found myself saying fatherly conservative things like, "This is not a training booklet," or "Maybe we should just skip on ahead to the next page."

The first sex scene panel had a comic book-like rendition of Edna Purviance about to go down on Chaplin's Charlie character. The bubble over Edna's head said, "There's nothing like ticklin' the little man in the boat." Attempting a comic footnote I added, "Today she'd probably have said, "Ticklin' the taco," or maybe "Dialing the 'zero' on the little pink phone. Stop me if I get unpleasant."

But Holly surprised me by offering up "How about 'scrubbing the cake pan'?" And then she shared a fittingly ribald film joke, "How did the grandmother of *Deep Throat*'s Linda Lovelace die? She went down on the *Titanic*." So much for protecting my daughter.

Returning to the first funny porno panel, the Tramp figure is very well endowed. The backdrop resembles the movie sets of the many short films done by Edna and Charlie. Consistent with Charlie's casual nature, he is reading the book *Easy Street* (the title of one of their best films together), while Edna is about to entertain the little fireman.

At this point the phone rang. It was way too late for telemarketers to annoy me. I cautioned Holly to not go on without me, and dashed to the next room to answer it. There was no response to my hello, though I could sense someone at the other end. My first thought was how ironically fitting — here we are looking at pornographic comics and now an obscene phone call. When nothing was forthcoming I merely hung up and thought no more about it. But when the same thing happened twice more that night, it only strengthened my resolve to soldier on regardless of intimidation tactics.

The second *Tijuana Bible* page had Charlie performing anal sex on Marion Davies in a castle-like setting, no doubt a reference to William Randolph Hearst's palace-sized home, San Simeon. The bubble over Charlie's head had him saying, "Hello, Hershey Highway."

"Okay Pop, what was this referred to back when you were a kid?"

"'Fudge packing' I believe, though I generally avoided the subject, if at all possible. Because I think this is what killed Moe and Curly. Larry I'm not so sure about."

With a comically grimacing expression Holly shared, "Well, you'll be happy to know it's not a major 'dear diary' item for me either. But to continue our kinky bonding process, I've heard it described as 'mud tunneling' and 'butt snorkeling.' Though I think my favorite is 'advanced leapfrog.'"

Laughing out loud at 'advanced leapfrog,' I added, "Who says parents and children don't talk anymore?"

The next page and panel was a bingo — Mildred Harris as Charlie's sexual partner. Probably inspired by Mildred's child-bride status, the comic strip background is a biology classroom. Charlie is a professor without pants, about to give Mildred an oral exam. She has her hair in pigtails and is wearing a convent school-like uniform. The bubble over Mildred's head has her saying "Give me a B's worth please," while Professor Charlie observes, "Hello, Miss Fur Pie." In the margin of the page someone had written, in a child-like scrawl, an alternative comment by Mildred — "Miss Fuzzy has been bad and needs a lickin'. "

The fourth page and panel also featured Mildred with Charlie. It is a courtroom setting with a stack of money on a table and the caption "100 G's." (This was the settlement amount she received in her divorce from Chaplin.) The comic-strip-styled Charlie is in a judge's robes but with an exposed and undersized Mr. Happy. The caricature of a scantily attired Mildred has her pointing at Charlie's "little fellow" and saying, "I don't do miniatures." Again, there was another handwritten alternative comment for Mildred in the margin, "Let's call this chapter, 'Sex Takes A Holiday.'"

The other four pages and pornographic panels in *Charlie Chaplin's Harem* showcased several other women in the comedian's life: second wife Lita Grey Chaplin; sometimes mistress and *Gold Rush* leading lady, Georgia Hale; the now legendary cult figure with the "Black Helmet" hair, actress Louise "Lulu" Brooks; and the famous period golddigger and sometime actress, Peggy Hopkins Joyce.

This second grouping of four was consistent with the comic-strip-styled pornography already described, though the Brooks panel featured the most entertaining dialogue bubble in this particular *Tijuana Bible*. That is, Charlie tearing his Tramp costume off while looking hungrily at a sexy Lulu. She, in turn, was innocently looking at the reader and saying, "He's really not bad, he just wants to be."

After having slowly gone through the whole booklet and saying very little, beyond the occasional exchange of sexual slang, or the popular "Holy Jesus shit," Holly and I sheepishly looked at each other and burst into laughter.

Finally, Holly managed to say, "Gee Dad, the things you expose your little girl to."

"That reminds me," I said. "When your Grandpa looked at these *Tijuana Bible*s in the 1930s, it was by way of a friend with an older brother —"

"That was their source?" asked Holly.

"Yeah, and I think the brother bought them out of the proverbial "backroom" of the local tobacco shop. Anyway, Grandpa and his friend would 'study' them in the nearest bathroom, behind the shower curtain."

"How old would they have been?" Holly asked.

"Eleven or twelve," I said. "Well, one day the friend's suspicious older sister surprises them in the bathroom. She rips open the shower curtain, grabs the booklet, and shouts at the top of her lungs, 'Mom, they're reading those fuckin' books again!'"

Laughing, Holly managed to ask, "Again?"

"It seems that Grandpa's sidekick had been caught once before, with another friend, examining a different *Tijuana Bible*." Sadly, this ended Grandpa's access to the world of *Eight Pagers*, at least until he was in the army."

"These were still floating around in the 1940s?" Holly asked.

"There was a war on. Soldiers had needs," I said.

"Yeah, right. So where's Evert's clue in all this?"

"I don't know. He said it was in the box. We'll just have to go back over everything until something clicks," I said.

"Is it okay if I keep trying to piece some of these newspaper fragments together?" Holly asked.

"Great. You'll need some glue. I'll get my box of desk supplies."

When I returned with the container she fished out the glue, as well as a magnifying glass. Putting the lens up to one eye, Holly mischievously said, "Hey, look at me. I'm Sherlock Holmes." Then she stood up and started loping around the room in a Groucho crouch, all the while holding the magnifying glass close to her right eye. "What's the film where the Marx Brothers are detectives?" she asked.

"*The Big Store*," I said. "Do you think we should call them in on the case?"

"No, I think I'll make more than enough comic blunders on my own," Holly answered. Returning to the table, she sat down and started in on her puzzle-like task. Without looking up she asked, "What are you going to do?"

"I'm going to reread everything until something jumps out at me," I said.

"It sounds like a plan," she answered. And for the next two hours we went about our tasks. Holly managed to piece together a *New York Herald Tribune* article entitled "Mildred Harris Chaplin Plays Helen Morgan." It was a vaudeville review that praised Mildred's impersonation of period singer Morgan. As with the other articles from Evert's box, it was dripping with irony. The Morgan song which Harris sang was "Those Little Things You Used To Do." Moreover, like Mildred, Morgan's screen career peaked early and she too scrambled to survive during the 1930s. When you factored in the item that both women were alcoholics who died young and at roughly the same time (early 1940s), one had a sad picture of Mildred's vaudeville act. She was earning a living through self-parody.

As ironically informative as this article was, the real find was the brief comment, "so far from *Oz*," someone had written in the left margin of the piece. It didn't resemble Evert's hand but when compared to Mildred's letter to Charlie we had a match.

"How sad," said Holly. "And so poetic, to make the *Oz* comparison."

"It might be more than a metaphor," I interjected.

"How do you mean, Pop?"

"Give me a second while I play reference librarian," I said. Pulling a film encyclopedia from a nearby shelf I looked up Harris' filmography. Flipping towards her citation I explained, "She started out as a child star."

"You saying she actually played an early Dorothy or something?" asked Holly.

"That's what I'm thinking Yeah, here we go," I said, finding the Harris citation. "At 13 she starred as Dorothy in four different silent film installments of *Oz*."

"Way to call it, Dad. Gee, I hope we don't find any *Tijuana Bible*s featuring Mildred and Toto."

"Please, you just gave me an image right up there with Bud Cort and Ruth Gordon's bedroom scene in *Harold and Maude*. I may have trouble getting an erection for the rest of my life."

This, of course, crossed a certain father/daughter line and Holly yelled, "Dad!" and proceeded to cup her hands over her ears and make whooping sounds which would have nicely complimented a Three Stooges film.

Eventually, we worked quietly for over an hour before I randomly shared, "If I could just figure out Evert's clue."

"No luck yet?" she asked.

"I've reread the articles until I'm blue in the face. Nothing. So I'm going to start going over our comic porn."

Laughing, Holly said, "Work, work, work." And then she began humming Gershwin's "Nice Work If You Can Get It."

Smiling, I observed, "Okay, okay. There might be worse duties." With that, Holly went back to her tweezer reconstruction chores and I again picked up *Charlie Chaplin's Harem*.

As I revisited *Tijuana Bible* land I kept trying to second guess where Evert would have placed his clue. As poignant and telling as the box's articles and letters were, firmly establishing that a Jesus picture had been shot by Chaplin, I decided that the clue had to be in this Charlie booklet.

I had three reasons to believe this. First, the *Tijuana Bible* was in the hidden compartment. Wouldn't you put the clue in the hardest to find spot? Second, while all the contents of Evert's box were fascinating, nothing was as provocative as this Charlie booklet. Again, wouldn't this be a perfect showcase for a clue? The only problem was

I couldn't find anything. The more I discovered, the less I knew. Third, if this lost Charlie picture was erotic, it would only be fitting that the clue was in the provocative *Tijuana Bible*.

Frustrated, I decided to play another hunch. If there was something to find in this comic porn *Harem*, I figured it would be on one of the two pages devoted to *Mildred* and Charlie. The biology classroom setting seemed a washout. But when I moved to the comic rendering of the two in court, I noticed something.

Holding the page up to the light prompted Holly to kiddingly ask, "Not nude enough for you?"

Ignoring her comment, I made a request, "Could you hand me that magnifying glass?" I had finally noticed what appeared to be a series of pin holes over several of the numbers and letters. Enlarging the holes definitely suggested they had been made with a message in mind.

Scanning the courtroom page from left to right there were, you should excuse the expression, pin pricks over each of the numbers in "100 G's." Mildred's comic dialogue, "I don't do miniatures," then offered pin holes above the following letters — n-o-t-e. And in the bottom right hand corner of the page, where the booklet title, *Charlie Chaplin's Harem* was repeated, there were pin pricks over the letters l-a-n-e. Putting all this together seemed to produce an address, 100 Note Lane.

Holly was quick to dig out a local city map from my kitchen junk drawer. There was a Note Lane in a section of Middletown known as "Old Town." Many historic buildings, both homes and businesses, in this area had been restored to all their early twentieth-century splendor.

"Let's go check it out," said an excited Holly.

Though equally pumped, I cautioned, "Who are you, Nora Charles? It's late, addresses are hard to find at night, and even if we track it down — we're not going to be able to do anything in the dark. Tomorrow I'll buy you a whole box of mystery novels and a DVD of *The Big Sleep*. Maybe for one of its extra features they'll have a behind the scenes look at a *Tijuana Bible* on Bogie."

But Holly was relentless, "Come on Pop, aren't you at least curious? We don't have to do anything tonight; I just want to drive by. . . ."

It was a perfect example of what comedian W. C. Fields once credited as being an "explanation as to why some animals eat their young." Still, she finally wore me down. "Okay, okay," I said. "I was afraid I was going to have to go to bed. But we're strictly casing the place. You have to promise me you'll make no attempt to get out of the car."

A comically solemn Holly immediately held up her right hand and said, "I'd rather destroy a stained glass window."

"Yeah, right," I answered.

We were soon in the car heading for "Old Town," about a fifteen minute drive. Having been built upon bluffs near the river, the area streets were extremely hilly. As we neared our address, we passed several of those buildings for which mudslides were invented. But nothing was going anywhere tonight.

100 Note Lane was almost more of an alley than a street. We missed our turn twice. But thanks to Holly's dexterity with the map and a pen light, we were soon driving by our address. And Evert could not have picked a more appropriate setting for clue number two. The exterior of 100 Note Lane was that of a restored early movie theatre, what had been once referred to as a "nickelodeon," based upon its inexpensive admission price. This was the type of place in which Chaplin's pioneering short subjects were first shown. With no cars in sight, we briefly parked across the street, and got out to take a good look.

The charmingly restored exterior now suggested that the one time nickelodeon was an entertainment-related gift shop. A tiny marquee proclaimed a name playing upon both the address and the Beatles — "PENNY LANE," followed by the phrase "Posters Plus." It would've looked inviting even if we weren't out looking for clues.

Holly and I had only been back in the car a few minutes when she noticed someone seemed to be following us. They were a block back or more but with literally nobody downtown at that time (after 2 a.m.), it was obvious they were mirroring our every move. I was tired and getting pissed; the badgering phone calls had shortened my fuse considerably. So I did a U-ie in the next intersection and started back towards our trailing car. It was anybody's guess what they'd do but they'd have to think fast, or we'd get a peek at them in the drive-by.

Not surprisingly, they turned off just in front of us. A glance at a nodding Holly told me what I needed to know — we followed the bad guys. It was a wonderful release after always being in the prey position. We were chasing a dark blue late model Buick, with a tree-sized dent, along the main drag out of the downtown. Heading west along the river towards the university the Buick accelerated to over seventy mph. Staying with them was no problem, but I started to ease up as we rapidly approached the campus. With Holly along I wasn't going to risk an accident. Plus, I neither had a gun, or a game plan. I was like that old gag about a weapon-less British Bobbie forced to shout, "Stop, or I'll yell, 'Stop,' again."

Dropping out of the chase was suddenly made easier by a flashing light. A university cop came up behind us and I pulled over. How the bad guys in the Buick got through this little speed trap I don't know. But it could have been worse, because the campus cop turned out to be Officer Roberts — who had written up my office break-in.

He started with the standard, "Do you know why I pulled you over?" bit, which they really do ask. But half-way through he recognized me, "Why Professor Caine, what's with the heavy foot? I just clocked you at over sixty in a thirty zone."

"We were following some people who maybe reorganized my office."

"You're kidding?"

"No, they were following us and we managed to turn the tables. Oh, Officer Roberts, this is my daughter Holly." She mouthed a silent "hi" and a small wave.

Roberts gave her a nodding smile and said, "Holly, I want you to police your old man. Any more high speed chases, however good the cause, and I'll have to haul him in."

Holly gave him a somber "Yes, sir."

Then turning to me he added, "Leave the police work to us, Professor. And the next time you think you have a lead, however thin, come see me." I made with the silent nod, and he started back to his patrol car. But then he stopped, and returned to my driver's side window. Forever the anxious type, *The Return of Roberts* (which would make a nice film title) was only making me nervous. As I again rolled down the window he said, "I meant to thank you before for donating those autographed books last month. They went over big at the charity auction. Bought one myself."

I managed a surprised, "Glad to help," and then he was gone. With our Charlie obsession now in fast forward mode, we still weren't ready to spill the unfolding Evert mystery with the police. And in all honesty, what are the authorities going to make of someone who starts ranting about a lost Charlie Chaplin porn picture, and the midget gangster out to get it? If that was my statement, (topped off with "What do you think of that?"), the cops' response would probably be, "Get back on the meds." But if and when the time came to talk, Roberts might be the man.

For the time being, however, Holly and I were both too tired for further reflection. We drove to my apartment and she crashed in the spare room. For once, late night writing wasn't even a consideration. I flopped down on my bed without bothering to undress. Let's just say I was going for that crumbled clothing look forever popular with low rent detectives and amateur sleuths. If it was a clothing line we'd call it the "*Columbo* Look."

Chapter 7

I am known in parts of the world by people who have never heard of Jesus Christ.
—Charlie Chaplin (circa 1925)

Not having had much sleep the previous night, I was a bit of a zombie the following morning at school. Department buddy Mark, with that perpetual gleam in his eye which suggested he knew something dirty that the rest of us didn't, was at his entertaining best trying to bring me back to the living. This translated into his telling an assortment of sex jokes. Popping into my office shortly after I arrived, he shared several stories along the following lines:

"How is American beer like making love in a canoe?"

"It's fucking close to water."

Thanks to Mark, several cups of industrial strength coffee, and teaching two classes, by early afternoon I was feeling almost alive again. I'd almost, at least momentarily, put the mystery of Evert out of my mind, when Mark came bursting into my office.

"It's that sexy number from Evert's memorial service," he said, breathless.

"Where?" I asked.

"In the outer office, bigger than life. And is she stacked. You could see them coming around the corner — give a guy time to comb his hair," he quipped.

"What's she doing here?" I asked.

"Who knows, or cares? Let's just be thankful for small favors. Well, actually big ones." At this point my phone rang, and after a brief conversation with the department secretary, I had an answer for Mark.

Hanging up the phone, I said, "It appears that Sexy Sadie has come to see me."

"No way," Mark said.

"Way. That was just Linda on the phone. Our mystery woman is a Ms. Hopper, and she's anxious to talk to me."

"What about?"

"Linda couldn't get that out of her," I said. "So I best go escort her back and see."

"You're my hero," said an affectionately mocking Mark. "I want a full report after you see her, and remember to use a rubber."

"Yeah, right."

After intros in the front office, and a casual stroll back to my office, Ms. Hopper and I were soon discussing the framed posters in my home-away-from home. She was darkly beautiful (cover girl stuff), with a serious mouth, come-fuck-me red lips, a thick helmet of hair (à la Louise Brooks), melon-sized breasts, long legs, and a direct come-hither gaze that was, well, sexy as hell. And yes, she would have been right at home in a Raymond Chandler novel, though if truth be told, I prefer Dashiell Hammett. Anyway, Ms. Hopper looked like a woman with a past. But as Oscar Wilde observed, most attractive women do.

"Thank you for seeing me," she said in a Bette Davis-like no-nonsense voice, coupled with penetrating Davis eyes.

"No problem," I answered, offering her a seat near my desk chair, which I then occupied. "Now, how can I help you?"

With a "State of the Union" seriousness she asked, "You were a friend of my uncle, Evert Harris?"

"Your uncle," I said, surprised.

"Yes, he was my mother's half-brother," she answered.

"Then Mildred Harris was —"

"My grandmother," she said. "While I never knew her, my mother was very dedicated to grandmother's memory."

"Is your mother still living?" I asked.

"No. That's why I've made it *my* task to carry on her mission."

"Mission?"

"To make the public aware of my grandmother's significance as a silent screen actress." Ms. Hopper said this with the overwrought zeal of a pastor looking for a hell to send someone to.

"Commendable, very commendable," I said. "But with 90 percent of all silent films lost, do you have enough Mildred Harris titles to make a case?"

"Quite frankly, no. But the family has always believed there was an unreleased Mildred Harris picture that, if found, would turn this all around." As she talked, she pulled on one of her ear lobes and I half expected her to go into some sort of Carol Burnett shtick.

Playing dumb (Holly would call it typecasting), I asked, "Where did the family get the idea about this film?"

"From grandmother herself," she said, without looking directly at me. Instead, her eyes were focused upon a miniature statue of Chaplin I had on my desk. Nodding towards it, and returning her gaze to me, she added, "She loved him so, and he just erased her from his life."

I answered her gently, "Just because you love something doesn't mean it has to love you back."

"Talent is a fragile thing," she said. "It's easily shattered by temperament, bad luck, and bad choices. Chaplin had a hand in all these things that brought her down."

"Hers is a sad story. But just about every funny figure I've written about was less than fun to live with."

"Then you're taking Chaplin's side?"

"It's not like that," I replied.

"Well, then what *is* it like?" she asked.

"When one studies art it is imperative to look beyond the personal liabilities of the artist."

"Oh, please, you professional appreciator. Now you sound like Evert," she said. "And he was part of the problem. . .her own son." She said these words in such a witchy manner (like someone had dropped a house on her sister), I couldn't help but think of Evert's violent death, and possibly the future headline, "Film Professor Bludgeoned to Death with Chaplin Statue."

"So how was Evert a problem?" I finally asked.

"As I'm sure you know, Chaplin is the one who produced my grandmother's unreleased movie."

"Let's assume for the sake of this conversation that there *was* such a movie, where does Evert fit into keeping it suppressed?" I asked, trying to maintain a lid on my immense curiosity.

"Evert was obsessed with Chaplin. Somehow he befriended the comedian's last wife—"

"Oona?"

"Yes, after Chaplin's death she became reclusive and alcoholic. Evert, under the auspices of doing a BBC documentary on silent comedy, somehow weaseled into her good graces, and obtained the missing movie."

My eyebrows did a quick jump to the ceiling and back as she watched me but my next question asked, "Given Evert's interest in Chaplin, and I assume in his own mother, why wouldn't he also want to bring this film to the public's attention?"

In the most coldly clipped pronouncement she said, "Evert never cared about Grandmother. Never."

Risking her anger, I softly offered a rebuttal to this position, "That wasn't quite my take on Evert."

"You even talked to him about his mother?" she asked with obvious surprise.

Counting the letters Evert shared from beyond the grave I quietly answered, "Yes, to me, he seemed to be just a son trying to come to grips with a mother who left him long before she died."

Ms. Hopper looked at me thoughtfully for a moment, "Hmm. Well, I guess we'll have to agree to disagree on that," she said, and without half the hostility I expected. "I thought you were just blowing smoke."

Since she seemed to be playing nice, I was encouraged to see how much she knew about the alleged Jesus slant of the Harris/Chaplin picture — "Just to play devil's advocate, let's take sabotage to grandmother's career out of the equation. Is there any other reason Chaplin might have shelved this alleged joint project?"

The beauty of the question, I thought, was that it also implied I knew less about the film. But as I waited for a Christ connection she floored me with the simple declaration, "The Jesus scenes were pornographic." ("Holy naked James M. Cain!" I thought to myself.)

"Pornographic?" I asked, stunned "According to whom?"

"My mother," she said, almost defensively.

"Sorry, I didn't mean to be so aggressive with the question. You just surprised me." In fact, I was still having problems processing the idea of a porno Jesus, played by Chaplin. The *Tijuana Bible* had really been an appropriate clue. Evert continued to be quite the card.

"What are you smiling about?" Ms. Hopper's voice suddenly interrupted my thoughts. "Cool down, Dr. Caine. By today's standards, we might only be talking an exposure rating of NC-17. All I know is that my grandmother had told my mother that there was nudity in it and yet, she felt good about the shooting just the same."

Bemused by a comment that sounded like an excerpt from a "Playmate of the Month" interview, I didn't say anything. In fact, neither of us said word one for a couple of minutes, until the silence in the room took on an insufferable Orson Welles-sized weight. It occurred to me at this point that Hopper was aptly named. Like a woman figure in a painting by Edward Hopper, she seemed trapped behind glass, despite a melancholy eroticism. Or, maybe Ms. Hopper wasn't so much under glass as she was looking at the world through a film noir window. She might also have been a visual metaphor for the collapse of the American Dream. But then maybe that's going too far. As George Carlin suggests, they just call it the American Dream because you have to be asleep to believe it.

Finally, surveying my movie poster-lined walls yet again, she asked in the most pleasant of tones, "Is it fair to assume that movies are your life?"

Following her gaze around my office I said, "I couldn't do anything else." Then, after a chuckle, I added, "No, I could be one of those farmers the government pays not to grow anything."

Ignoring my joke, and making direct eye contact, she said in a vulnerable, almost sexy whisper, "You'll hate me for asking this."

Smiling this time, she suddenly stood up (her body all high-breasted alertness), and took what was no more than the single step that separated us. Half expecting her to pull a weapon, I too stood up as a defense mechanism. Instead, she nestled into my body like we were going to dance. Planting her thighs against mine and wrapping those sleeve-less arms around me, she delivered an open-mouthed kiss. As her tongue massaged the inside of my mouth I couldn't help thinking that if this were a movie the soundtrack number would be "Steam Heat."

As much as I'm in favor of beautiful women massaging my gums (let the good times begin), when it does occur I'm always suspicious. See, I've already had one of those mornings where you look in the mirror and realize you're not going to die young. Thus, I knew there had to be an ulterior motive going on. Though I was tempted to recycle my all-time favorite Bob Hope line, "Don't ever leave me Baby, you'd suffer."

Not surprisingly, when she finally pulled back from her seminar in smooching (everyone needs air eventually), she had a proposition for me. Join her, whatever that meant, and there would be more than just tonsil hockey going on.

"Sorry but no," was my answer. Then I threw in a line from a movie I'd always wanted to use, "I wouldn't be any more help than a melted candle." (I forever try to bring a little class to my dialogue.)

I figured she'd get pissy over my turning her down, but instead she snuggled back against me and said, "I don't understand."

Now I have no way of knowing if this ploy of being incredibly stupid normally works. But I wasn't buying. Instead, I replied in kind, "No can help. Evert friend. Me not have lost film. Hate midget in yellow."

Bingo, she slapped me, and said, "That's some cold shit. What d'ya teach here, classes in nasty?"

I had to give Ms. Hopper credit, her little indignant performance was good, not to mention the great wrist action in that slap. I only wish I'd had some prop teeth in my mouth to spit back. But since I'd left them in my other jacket, I did the next best thing — I slapped her, which further infuriated Ms. Hopper. But before we were reduced to the take-your-turn, tit-for-tat violence of a Laurel & Hardy routine, there was a knock on my slightly ajar office door.

Suddenly Holly casually leaned her head and shoulder through the door opening and offered the easygoing greeting, "Hello? I'm here to help."

"Do you have a gun?" I dryly responded.

That comment elicited an angry comeback from Hopper, "You'll think gun," as she brusquely pushed by Holly and stormed out.

Holly surveyed my office before stepping in, as if to check for other angry women. "Brrr, a dip of Rocky Road wouldn't have melted on her. What brought all that on?"

"Probably low blood sugar," I said.

Smiling, she affectionately pushed my shoulders and demanded, "Seriously?"

"She wanted me to join forces in finding a certain Chaplin film."

"And?" asked Holly.

I don't trust her any further than I can throw a Buick. So I turned her down. Except she wasn't taking no for an answer."

"Maybe it was more than that," said Holly. "How did Mark Twain say it, 'Denial ain't just a river in Egypt.'"

Now it was my turn to smile, and I kidded her by asking, "Have you been mixing your cereal with crack again?"

With a silly smile, and a tilt of her head she said, "You ask that like it's a bad thing." And then she let go with one of her great laughs. Holly has the best laugh in the history of all-time laughs.

After this pleasant distraction, I couldn't help returning to the subject of Ms. Hopper. "Denial complexities or not, that woman needs to choke up on reality. I wouldn't be surprised if she had something to do with the demise of our late, great professor."

"You mean Evert Harris?! I didn't know you were an expert on murder," said Holly, suddenly playing at being serious. Picking up a note pad and pencil from my desk, she did a broad imitation of a reporter covering a press conference. "You know, I would take better notes. But getting a story in my paper is the same as putting it in a bottle and pitching it in the sea. Still, Mr. Professor, you think there's a connection with this murder?"

Waving her off I said, "It's like your grandmother used to say, 'You don't have to be a hen to know a bad egg.'"

I had no sooner said 'bad egg' than Hopper was back in the doorway. Preparing to say something sarcastic, I was suddenly taken aback by the saddest of faces. She looked like Bambi, just after the hunting story broke.

"I came back to apologize Professor. My temper gets the better of me sometimes."

Holly, who was out of Ms. Hopper's line of sight (behind my door), caught my attention with a wave of her hand. She then mouthed the word:

B-I-P-O-L-A-R

Ignoring my homegrown stand-up comic I replied, "That's okay, I've been known to fly off the handle myself." Holly nodded in silent agreement — much too quickly for my tastes.

"But I am glad I came back," said Ms. Hopper. "There's so much more I'd like to go over. Could we meet again, if I promise to be good. . .maybe at my hotel — the Rivera. Shall we say Friday at eight?"

"We can say it. I don't know what it means, but we can say it."

"You're such a kidder Dr. Caine. But seriously, it would mean so much to me." And between those pouting lips and the chance to find out more about Mildred, I found myself making a date with Evert's sexy niece. Off to my right Holly could only shake her head.

Chapter 8

Chaplin was so popular in the 1910s and 1920s that a theatre was guaranteed sold-out numbers by simply putting a cardboard cutout of Charlie on display which simply said, "I am here today."

"What could you have been thinking?" asked Holly, as soon as the coast was clear. "The woman doesn't have all her buttons. She's fuckin' jumped the tracks."

"I'll just pump her for some information."

"Yeah, you'll pump her alright. Dad, she's a predator. I mean, we're talking 'Femme Fatale 101.' She's another Barbara Stanwyck in *Double Indemnity*."

"P-l-e-a-s-e! Don't compare me to Fred MacMurray. Personally, I don't know what Billy Wilder was thinking casting MacMurray—"

"Don't change the subject, Pop. Besides, you're the one that showed me *Double Indemnity* when I was seven, for crying out loud. All my friends were talking about the latest Disney picture and you're giving me a film noir tutorial. Is it any wonder I worry about you?"

I swallowed hard and gave her a smile. "Okay point taken. Maybe I've just got caught up in our little adventure. Danger for me doesn't usually involve anything more scary than a paper cut, or the occasional stress involved with wanting to brain a student."

"I know what you're saying, Dad. Lately I feel like someone trying to be calm on one of the drop rides, just before the free fall."

At this point we took a time-out and discussed everything, from my tentative rendezvous with Ms. Hopper, to the Buick that nearly made us deader than a squashed squirrel. Should we continue? Holly joked about simplifying her wardrobe by buying a shirt with a bull's eye on the back. We even flirted with telling the whole story to the police. But ultimately, we decided to continue our personal crusade (whatever that involved) to find the *Time Machine* film. It was a classic example of having invested too much time and effort to back off. Plus, the excitement, and even the danger, was pretty heady stuff. I was reminded of an old *New Yorker* cartoon where a druggy says, "Rehab is for quitters."

Having reached this decision, Holly and I made a beeline for Penny Lane, with an even more cautious lookout for big, blue Buicks. The front part of the store was in what had evidently been the lobby of the old theatre. The room was devoted almost exclusively to posters. They were on the walls, in bins, and spread out on tables.

The original posters were individually mounted on linen and stacked in inviting piles, by genre, on various tables. We surveyed the layout for some time before a voice from the next room said, "What can I do you for?" God, I hate that expression.

Soon an overweight, geriatric hippie type with a Steven Seagal ponytail and a tie-dyed T-shirt came bouncing into the room. He seemed a little hyper and inbred, like my cousin Stewart. There was also something blurry about his kisser, as if the powers that be (film noir fatalism) hadn't decided what kind of mug he should have. Of course, this isn't to be confused with the soft-focus squishiness you experience in a romantic movie. Though, speaking of that genre, this fellow also rather reminded me of the character who collected discarded photos in the French film *Amelie* — another marginal soul in search of a more focused identity. He was what prostitutes would call a "cash upfront customer." When he repeated his inane question ("What can I do you for?"), it was all I could do to keep from smacking him in that blurry mug.

Instead, I asked, "Do you have any Chaplin posters?"

"Reprints or originals?" he replied.

"You have originals?" I said, impressed.

"We have some of the late stuff, like *Limelight* and *A King in New York*, as well as the reissue titles, after he did his Oscar thing."

"Thanks," I said. "We'll maybe just look around."

"Sure, be my guest. We've only been open a few days, so if you don't mind, I've got some odds and ends to do in back."

"What's the next room?" I asked.

"That's 'Charlie's Place,'" he said.

"Pardon me?"

"Oh, sorry. We're refurbishing the building's old theatre. And we've named it 'Charlie's Place,' after Chaplin."

"How'd you decide on 'Charlie'?" I asked.

"Well, we had a generous patron, and that was his one stipulation. Would you like the nickel tour?"

So Holly and I joined him in "Charlie's Place." And it reflected everything I'd read about those pioneering nickelodeon theatres. A small narrow room with backless wooden benches for about forty people. Plus, the antique projector was simply in the back of the room, as was then the norm, as opposed to today's separate booth.

As we followed our hippie host around the room I asked, "Was your benefactor Evert Harris?"

That stopped Mr. Tie-Dyed in his tracks. In response to the startled look he shot my way I explained, "Evert was a friend of mine. I used to teach with him at the college."

"Is your name Caine?" he asked.

Now it was my turn to be surprised. "How did you know?" I said.

"Let's just say you were not entirely unexpected. Will you excuse me for a minute?"

After he left the room Holly rubbed her hand over a knothole in one of the benches and asked, "What did all that mean?"

"I don't know. But it looks like we got the address right," I said.

Tie-dyed came back shortly and shared, "Someone wants to meet you."

I focused more closely on his blurry mug and tried to get a "read" on where he was coming from but he seemed to be strictly a messenger type. With a smile I replied, "Nobody scary I hope. This person doesn't eat puppies or anything?" I asked. "Or drive a beat-up blue Buick perchance?"

Laughing, our hippie clerk said, "Not that I know of."

"Do you have an address?"

"No need to. A car is on the way."

This produced a worried glance from Holly but no brain hemorrhage or anything. Still, with everything that had happened, I wasn't planning on biting that easy. But I played along, asking, "How'd we get to be the luckiest folks in this postal district?"

"I couldn't really tell you," he said. "I'm just sort of a traffic cop here, I try to keep people from bumping into each other."

"And Mr. Constable, just where is it that we're going?" I asked.

"I think that's supposed to be a surprise," he said.

"Unfortunately," I shared, "Holly and I tend to avoid surprises. We have this thing about a full itinerary."

Looking concerned, like he'd misplaced his laminated Woodstock tickets, he said, "If it's any comfort to you, I think it's okay to tell you that this is part of the puzzle Evert created for you."

Holly caught my gaze and gave me a shrug of her shoulders. Then, almost simultaneously, we both turned our eyes towards Hippie Boy.

This sudden attention produced an expression that seemed to say, "I'm the last person in the world that would be part of hurting someone."

About the time I expected him to pull out a handkerchief, the front door of the shop opened and a chauffeur type cautiously stepped in, like the building wasn't up to code. Without so much as a look in any direction he enunciated my name into the most world weary question imaginable, "P-r-o-f-e-s-s-o-r C-a-i-n-e?" He gave off such an odor of indifference you could feel your confidence draining just being near him.

I didn't know whether to respond to this motorized Jeeves, or pull his chain with silence. But not wanting to come across as some sort of class warrior, I quickly owned up to being me. Jeeves was soon ushering Holly and me out, and as we looked back at Hippie Boy one last time he, believe it or not, gave us the peace sign.

Outside the longest stretch limo (we're talking multiple time zones) this side of Donald Trump awaited us curbside. Even as Jeeves opened the door I had no plans on our getting in. But then he said a curious thing. "Mr. Schickel does not like delays of any kind."

"That wouldn't be James Schickel, would it?" I asked.

"One and the same," he answered.

"Okay Holly, change of plans. We're going for a ride." She gave me a quizzical look but piled into the limo after me.

Once inside, however, it was, "What gives, Pop?"

"Schickel is one of the country's biggest collectors of movie memorabilia. But he's a real recluse, sort of the J. D. Salinger of poster art."

"He lives around here?" Holly asked.

"Well, not quite. It's somewhere between here and Chicago, maybe two or three hours. He's not exactly in the phone book — recluses are funny like that. I've been trying to touch bases with him forever. . .and now we get his limo! Maybe God, at last, is starting to balance the books."

"Okay," Holly said. "Just to recap. We're not going to die. Right? Would that be a fair assessment?"

Ignoring this, I said, "You know, when Evert accepted the endowed chair, having Schickel in the state was supposedly a factor."

"Then they were friends?" asked Holly.

"Well, Evert was always sort of vague on that. But given this latest twist, it would seem like it."

"All right, that clears it up for me, I can relax now." And with that, Holly stretched back in what was essentially a large playroom on wheels. There were two bars (front and back), a fridge, and a DVD projection system. Near our wrap-around seating in the rear there was also a DVD storage trunk which included a complete run of Chaplin titles.

As the limo seemed to accelerate (we'd probably reached the beltway) I asked Holly, "Well, what d'ya think?"

"It beats the bus," she said. "Except, what's with the windows?" In what amounted to a reverse tint, we couldn't see out.

"We'll just assume it's better for viewing the movies," I replied.

With a big grin on her face she said, "Nothing like adding more mystery to our mystery. I wonder if Evert sat up nights putting this all together?"

In a playful mood I suggested a travel game, "Maybe we could piece together exactly where we're going by the sounds we hear along the way. You know, like in that Robert Redford film.

"*Sneakers,*" she said. "Let's not and say we did. I think that kind of stuff only works in the movies."

Watching her stretch out among an assortment of pillows I observed, "It's good to see you taking this lying down."

Smiling, she said, "Yes, there's nothing like a little detective work to help you chill out." Then she mimed doing her nails.

"How about a little refreshment for your traveling pleasure?" I asked, as I slid myself across a cushioned path to the bar. Retrieving a Coke for Holly and a Coors Lite for myself, I had soon followed her lead and stretched out in our little traveling oasis. I think this was a pretty strong case against Tolstoy's claim that the only true happiness comes from hard work and sacrifice. But to commemorate our road trip we decided to put on Chaplin's ultimate road picture — *Modern Times*. After that we watched a couple Charlie short subjects, only to be jarred back into the conversation mode by rough road conditions.

"What gives?" Holly asked. "Daddy, tell the operator I want the ride to stop."

"We appear to have turned onto the mother of all gravel roads," I explained. "When I was a kid we used to call rough spots like this 'washboard.'"

"Thanks for that pithy flashback, Dad. Now make it stop," Holly requested. "If this handheld camera effect doesn't stop soon I'm going to be sick."

As if a wish had been granted the roadbed suddenly smoothed out. Soon we were slowing down and making a sharp turn. Then we came to a slow stop and there was the sound of several barking dogs close around the car.

"Great," said a big eyed Holly, "Schickel brought us here to be eaten by canines. Maybe our Chaplin adventure should be re-titled, 'Charlie Meets Cujo.'"

At that precise moment the limo door was opened from outside and a blinding wave of sun light washed over us. It was like when you sit up too quickly and that starry cloud of diamonds condenses around your head.

From outside the limo, it no doubt seemed like there was a problem. But we had remained planted strictly out of blindness. Then the kindest, gentlest voice floated into the car, "Is everything okay, Professor Caine?"

"Not to worry," I managed, as Holly and I climbed out of the limo cocoon.

Once I could see straight I was in for a major surprise. I'm sure my now big eyes and opened mouth made me look like a treeful of owls. Our apparent host was the spitting image of the late great Evert. I momentarily thought my old colleague had pulled a fast one on me. Acknowledging my startled expression, the Evert lookalike introduced himself with, "I'm James Schickel, and yes, I could've been Professor Harris' twin."

Leading Holly and me up a gravel path to a two-story limestone farmhouse, we were soon in what could have passed for an art gallery. The first floor interior had been gutted into one large rectangular room, approximately 90 feet by 30 feet, with a metal spiral staircase in the center. The white textured walls were covered with framed vintage film posters. We were definitely in movie connoisseur country. And he let us linger there for a heavenly half hour.

Promising us a bite to eat, Schickel then took us to the second floor, which was broken into three rooms, a large film library, what appeared to be a bedroom area, and a bar/kitchenette. Leading us directly to the latter room, a deli-like smorgasbord of cold cuts, salads, and assorted breads had seemingly been laid out for us. Inviting Holly and me to help ourselves he planted himself in a corner wicker chair, content to watch us chow down. A refrigerator hummed to itself in the background.

Starting to make a pocket sandwich, I told Schickel, "I always appreciate an abductor who sets a tasty table. It shows a nice spirit."

"It's the least I can do for your inconvenience." Like Evert, he wore a bow tie and favored clothes from another era. "Please forgive my cloak and dagger style. I've gotten caught up in Evert's gamesmanship. We were acquaintances for many years, which was unusual for me. You see," he said with a twinkle in his eyes, "I miss companionship — as much as I can. Anyway, I promised Evert this would come off without a hitch."

"So what's coming off?" I asked.

"Well, if memory serves, I've got a package for you in the library," said Schickel.

"It's not tickin', is it?" I asked.

"Oh, it's a bomb alright, but not the kind you mean. More on the order of a bombshell," said Schickel.

"How so?" I asked, between nibbles on my sandwich.

"Well, obviously, I'm a collector. That's how I met Evert — outbid him on a *Big Sleep* full sheet poster some years back. Anyway, I don't mind telling you, most movie folks I know would sell their soul for a chance at this Evert surprise."

"So when do we get to play Christmas?" I asked.

"Hold your horses, Professor. Finish your sandwich, and I'll get the package."

With Schickel's exit, Holly smiled and said, "So, Father of mine, what do you think Evert has got in store for us this time around?"

"You got me, Kiddo, but it ought to be good. He hasn't let us down yet."

"Dad, did you get a load of this *Duck Soup* poster?" Just to the right of Holly was a framed full sheet of the Marx Brothers' classic. The only other one I had ever seen was in the film archive at the Library of Congress. To paraphrase a line from Woody Allen, "I'd sell my mother to the Arabs for that poster." The kitchen area had several food related posters, including another Groucho and company full sheet — *Animal Crackers*.

Kiddingly I told Holly, "Why don't you cause a diversion and I'll make a break for it with *Duck Soup*."

"You're busted," said a smiling Schickel, who reentered the kitchen at this exact moment.

Mildly embarrassed, I shared, "I did my dissertation on McCarey [the director of *Duck Soup*] and —"

"Forget it," said an amused Schickel. "There isn't a collector alive who hasn't contemplated a little grand larceny. But for the moment you've got bigger fish to fry." He then placed a worn leather satchel in my hands. Embossed on the leather flap were some familiar icons, a pair of worn shoes, a battered derby, and a little cane. And they were done in a manner which mirrored Chaplin's once famous and elaborate autograph, which also included all these figures.

With nervous hands I opened up the satchel and pulled out a thumb-worn sheaf of papers, perhaps forty unnumbered pages, with the title *Charlie Chaplin and the Time Machine* typed at the top of each one. A cursory examination of the pages suggested this was Mildred Harris' portion of the script.

Schickel broke into my thoughts with the comment, "You'll be wanting to get back and give that the once over. So I'll see you to the car." No one said word one on the walk back to the limo. Recluses seldom tend to be chatty. I did run one poster question by him, unrelated to our Evert mystery. But Schickel seemed about as interested in my modest inquiry as I was in the mating habits of the Duck-Billed Platypus, so I let it slide.

Once at the car, however, Schickel affectionately shook our hands, like a long lost uncle, and wished us "Godspeed," the first time I'd heard that expression outside of a novel. I thanked him for his help and joked, if I was ever in the neighborhood. . .I wouldn't know it. He smiled and clapped me on the shoulder, like my joke had endorsed his mysterious manner of getting us there — wherever *there* was. Unless he was just fucking with me. As an insecure type, I frequently log time wondering if people are fucking with me. My James Thurberish shrink blames it on my having measles as a child, also my excuse for not being able to dance. (Strict Freudian therapists sometimes use humor in lieu of answers.) Evert's murder had done nothing to increase my confidence in either "reading" a person, or psychiatry in general. Of course, I'm not suggesting a massacre of shrinks either. . .at least not at the present time.

Regardless, Schickel packed Holly and me in his cocoon-mobile and sent us back to the city. Before his use of the antiquated "Godspeed," which went so well with his bow tie and other era clothing, he'd entertainingly revealed the ongoing temptations of being a collector, "You best get going before I further ponder just what it is I'm giving up." Consistent with that, Holly and I could not wait to get at Mildred's portion of the script — of a movie that now seemed unbelievably real.

Chapter 9

Everyone has their reasons.
— Jean Renoir, celebrated director and Chaplin aficionado

At the risk of getting dizzy as a pair of loons, Holly and I started reading the Chaplin script before we were out of Schickel's farm yard. I'd eyeball a page and then I'd pass it to Holly. We were through what turned out to be thirty-five pages in thirty minutes.

The silent film script excerpt anticipated by decades the novel *The Last Temptation of Christ*, which was later movingly adapted to the screen by Martin Scorsese. That is, when Chaplin, as Jesus, is on the cross He imagines what his life would have been like had He been allowed to lead a normal life. Most specifically, this involved marriage over the ministry. Since Scorsese's 1988 adaptation was controversial, one can just imagine the response Chaplin would have received in the 1920s — sort of a *cross* between the Spanish Inquisition and a KKK cookout.

Chaplin/Jesus' "wife" was the woman (prostitute) at the well, Mary Magdalene, to be played by Mildred. Consequently, the script's detailed sex scene was played in the context of the two being married. While there was no way around the still provocative nature of any love scene involving Christ, much of the other domestic material in this *Time Machine* script was played for laughs. But this was hardly surprising, given that Chaplin was playing Jesus. These Mildred-directed scenes were not unlike Chaplin's later domestic fantasy in 1936's *Modern Times*, where the Tramp and the Gamin (Paulette Goddard) set up housekeeping. For example, in *Modern Times* there is an orange tree so close to the house that Charlie can pick fruit from the window. In the *Time Machine* script, the easy-access fruit was a fig tree, which was more in keeping with the Middle East. Otherwise, both scenes played the same. Indeed, another *Modern Times* bit of domestic shtick — where a nearby cow produces milk by way of a mere pat on the back — was mapped out verbatim in the earlier *Time Machine* script. (Comedy in Scorsese's version was strictly unintentional, such as Harvey Keitel's Judas speaking with a New York accent.)

Chaplin also wrote comedy material related to Christ being a carpenter, with His shop attached to the house. Mildred's Mary doubled as an antiheroic assistant forever screwing up whatever Chaplin's Jesus asked her to do. One script direction had Christ looking at the camera with comic exasperation, following more loopy behavior by Mary/Mildred. One wonders if Oliver Hardy had access to any of this, because he would later use the same sort of frustrated direct address when Stan Laurel would get them in "another fine mess."

Of equal interest was a compendium of scene synopses which involved Chaplin's second role in the film — where he joins Jesus as a time-tripping *13th* disciple. There was no ready explanation as to why these thumbnail sketches should appear with Mildred's pages, too. But her character did seem to surface in several of the scenes. Regardless, this Biblical Charlie the Tramp, this "13th disciple," was used by Chaplin as a catalyst for pivotal events in the life of Jesus. For instance, in the scriptures according to Chaplin, Christ's trashing of the temple moneylenders was precipitated by a clumsy Charlie. That is, the Tramp accidentally hooked his cane on some scales used for weighing gold, causing him to accidentally strip the top of a moneylender's table.

Chaplin's Jesus took the result of Charlie's errant cane as a spontaneous act of conscience by his 13th disciple, and acted accordingly. But even Christ's anger at the misuse of His Father's house had a comic Chaplin flair. When his Jesus attempts to overturn one moneylender's table (which, unbeknownst to him, is bolted to the floor), he cannot budge it, despite the muscle-quivering assistance of Charlie. This results in Jesus and the Tramp hurriedly exiting the scene on skidding sandals, only to quickly return with axes, with which they quickly reduce the table to so much kindling.

The most comically poignant scene which involved these three principals (Jesus, Mary, and Charlie) was when Chaplin as Christ saved Mary from being stoned by a mob. The comedian as Jesus passionately pantomimes the spiel, "let he who is without sin cast the first stone" (which the script also noted would be on a title card). Though the crowd seems to have been placated, a small angelic-looking child then beans Chaplin as Christ on the head with a pebble, causing him to "comically stumble about with a stunned expression."

(The scene closes with the comedian as Jesus paddling this little Biblical brat.)

Interestingly enough, this beaning was probably the model for a 1940 *Great Dictator* scene, where Charlie's sweetie (again Paulette Goddard) accidentally smacked him with a frying pan. The result was the most inspired of dazed dances, which might have been tentatively entitled "Seeing Stars." Coupled with the *Time Machine* script's aforementioned domestic scenes, this Chaplin screenplay appeared to have been the starting point for several later signature sketches by the silent comedian. Now it was just a matter of seeing how much of this Chaplin had committed to film. All this and more was a lot to process. When I passed the last page to Holly I laid my head back and closed my eyes.

"Wow! We've got to find this movie!" Holly had finished the script. "What do you think? Some read, huh?!"

Without opening my eyes I answered, "Damn straight. If even a fraction of this is on film we're on to the biggest lost movie ever. But we be fucked if we can't come up with the next clue."

"Shit! I forgot about that. But you're good, Dad. For crying out loud, you found pin points in that *Tijuana Bible*. Besides, this latest installment of the mystery came with a limousine. I think the lord will provide —"

"Or Mr. Schickel," I said. "Speaking of limos, what time is it? It's at least another two hours, right? I hate these reverse tinted windows, not being able to see out."

"Who's paranoid now? Relax. We've got real script pages from a lost Charlie movie! There is a God and he's a Chaplin fan! Now if we can just get the next clue.

"Amen to that. I continue to be concerned over what I got you into. . .[pause]. You know novelist Michael Chabon?"

"The guy who wrote *Wonder Boys*? Holly asked.

"Yeah. He once said that film addicts climb into a movie as if it were a time machine and set the dial for 'never come back.'"

"Cool. I like that," said Holly.

"Me too. That's how I feel about this lost film. I won't be happy until we get it. And even then I probably won't be happy because unlike the character in Woody Allen's *Purple Rose of Cairo*, I haven't quite mastered crossing over into a movie yet."

"Pop, have you been smoking funny cigarettes again?" joked Holly.

"No, but what I'm about to say will probably make you think so."

"How's that?" asked Holly.

"Did you ever look in the mirror so long your mug stopped making sense, like you got too close to an Impressionist painting? Well, I think maybe we've gotten too close on this Chaplin case. Maybe we should just step back, take a deep breath, and let some more conventional problems cause the cardiac arrest."

"But Pop, this is nothing a roof top and an AK-47 wouldn't take care of."

"My thoughts exactly," I said. Before I could say more, slow-talking Jeeves opened the compartment portion separating us and said, "There seems to have been an accident up ahead with a Little Debbie delivery truck. What would you advise I do?"

"Is anyone hurt?" I asked, since Holly and I still couldn't see out.

"Someone appears to be lying along the shoulder."

"By all means, stop," interjected Holly.

So we pulled off the side of the road and Jeeves was soon opening the door for Holly and me. As we got out, Schickel's man had the most quizzical look on his face, like he had found a finger in his root beer, or some such thing. But before I could even hazard a guess I had an answer — the midget in yellow was back, and he was waving a gun, like he'd just come from a James Cagney seminar.

The little shit looked pleased with his fake accident trap, like someone had died and appointed him mayor of fun-ville. We were still out in the country — on a deserted piece of road. And we'd been suckered by a midget with a Little Debbie delivery truck. Who knows, maybe the shrimp was related to Little Debbie. At the moment there was a woman behind the wheel of the truck. But I couldn't tell if it was Evert's gun-toting niece.

"So Professor, how's it hangin'?" said the economy-sized villain. Gesturing towards Holly he asked, "Is this your daughter, or are you robbing the cradle?"

Ignoring this, I went for the insult, borrowing a line from W. C. Fields, "Are you standing in a hole?"

"Gee, Professor, you allow very little wiggle room. I was hoping maybe you missed me. How big a hurt are you nursing?"

"So big it should have orange cones and police tape around it," I said. "But I mean that in a good way."

Chuckling, the little man observed, "That's what I like about you, Professor. I always know where I stand with you. So, you maybe ready to come over to our side?"

"Let me put it to you in movie terms, I'm not really interested in having a great part in a film that's not very good. It's like being the head flea on a dead dog."

"I'll take that as a no."

"WHAT DO YOU WANT WITH US?" The midget and Jeeves and I all visibly jumped. Holly had fairly shouted this at this refugee from *The Wizard of Oz*. She was somewhere between scared and pissed. Trading cracks with short stuff, I'd half forgotten she was there, and I guess the other two had also. "Why didn't you jump us back at Schickel's?" Holly asked.

"She's good," said the midget. Turning to my daughter he answered, "Schickel's place might look like something out of Grant Wood but it's a fortress, with lots of people behind the scenes. Anyway, I want whatever Schickel gave you, and I want it now."

"What if the answer is no?" said Holly with the accent now definitely on pissed. (Jeeves made a whimpering sound.) Holly had her arms crossed and was in what I used to call her "defiant mode," a pose she'd been assuming since the age of two.

Scratching his forehead with the barrel of a nickel plated .38, the bemused shrimp told Holly, "I guess the apple never falls far from the tree. But I'll cut you some slack, Sugar, and forget I heard that, what with you looking like a doll who might turn up in my dreams."

"I don't think so," said Holly. "I'm particular what kind of dreams I find myself in."

"I love it." Looking at me he added, "She's got a lot of moxie, Professor. But tell her playtime is over now." His gun was back at waist level, pointed at me.

Slowly turning to Holly I asked in the most measured manner, "Would you get the script for me?"

Without taking her eyes off our undersized problem, she asked, "Are you sure, Dad?"

"Yeah honey, he's holding all the cards. . .and a gun. Get it for me."

Slowly and reluctantly Holly climbed back in the limo and gathered up Mildred's script pages from the back seat. So much for us finding more movie clues on the whereabouts of Chaplin's lost film. As if reading my mind, and before Holly handed me the script, she held a couple pages up to the light, no doubt hoping for some sort of sign to unlock the mystery location of a film called *Charlie Chaplin and the Time Machine*.

When nothing magical occurred, she had to settle for a darkly comic wish when she handed me the pages, "Jeeves should have just made him a road bump."

Smiling in agreement, I took the script from her and started to hand it over to our littlest gangster, who had actually taken a step towards me in anticipation of getting his stubby fingers on it. But a funny thing happened on the way to coughing up the Chaplin script.

The worm turned (that would be me). Don't ask me why. Maybe it was my daughter's disappointment at giving the pages up, and my concern that her disappointment carried over to me. Maybe it was my reluctance to part with something that had belonged to my personal hero (all hail Charlie). Maybe it was seeing too many of Errol Flynn's swashbuckling epics as a child. Or, maybe it was simply some macho thing about not taking any crap from someone the size of a third grader.

Whatever the reason, I was about to do something very foolish. I used to think my life would pass before my eyes in a situation like this. But I was too afraid. Still, there was no resisting this sudden death-wish to act like a movie hero. So what happened?

Well, as our Tom Thumb tough guy walked towards me with his hand outstretched he made the mistake of once again scratching his forehead with the barrel of his .38. He then added to his vulnerability by only having eyes for the script. So while he was distracted in getting Mildred's pages from my left hand, I clocked him with my open hand — jamming the barrel hard into his forehead.

He went down like a ton of bricks (well, a half ton in his case), assuming a state not unlike whiskey coma. Taking no chances, however, I relieved him of his .38, while he slept the sound sleep of someone knocked silly. It all happened so fast that Holly practically missed it. But whoever was at the wheel of the Little Debbie truck had been paying attention, because they were burning rubber practically before the shrimp hit the ground.

Having seen all of Bogie's tough guy detective movies, I decided to frisk Sleeping Beauty, especially since he continued to lay there like a slug. It turned out his name was Bob Evans — no kidding — and his P. I. License (yes, he was a certified little dick) had a Queens address, Flushing Meadows (Archie Bunker territory).

Business must have been good for Bob, what with fifteen crisp one hundred dollar bills in his billfold, and an assortment of tens and twenties. I initially planned to take it all as payback for past aggravation but then I thought better of it, and left him five dollars.

Meanwhile, Holly was bouncing up and down like someone on a basketball highlight reel who has just canned a game winning three-pointer. Even Jeeves, our less than demonstrative driver, was sporting a broad grin. Score one for the professor.

Our celebration was cut short by Bob showing moaning signs of coming to. Moving closer to the horizontal hoodlum for the first time, Holly asked, "So what's our plan for him?" Getting a wicked smile on her face she added, "I vote we hurt him some more."

"First, let's see if we can pump him for information," I said. By splashing him with mineral water Jeeves had volunteered from the limo, we soon had him back among the living.

"What hit me?" he asked, as his eyes panned the three people standing over him.

"I'm afraid I used your gun," I said, which I was holding on him to maintain the advantage.

"Ohhh," he said, as he gingerly touched the Warner Brothers cartoon sized lump which was beginning to form on his little pointy head.

"We hoped you might fill in a few blank spots for us," I asked.

Slowly getting to his feet, he just looked at us.

"For starters," said Holly, "are you working for the Hopper woman?"

Looking the three of us over one more time, with almost a hurt look in his eyes, Bob's gaze stopped at the .38. When he finally spoke he seemed to direct his answer at the gun, as if it had become a fifth member of the group, "I don't have anything to share with anybody."

Then, as if to second that notion, a shot rang out from a stand of trees about fifty yards behind Bob, and his head exploded in our faces.

Chapter 10

When the world looks grim and dark, then I think of another world.
                              — Chaplin's Monsieur Verdoux *(1947)*

When Bob's head exploded, none of us wasted any time diving behind the limo. Survival is funny that way. When no more shots rang out, our man Jeeves motioned for us to crawl to the front passenger side door and get in.

As Holly made her way over like a soldier on all fours, I detoured by the splattered remains of the midget and retrieved Mildred's portion of the script. Even without a head he didn't want to give up the pages. I had to literally pry them out of his death grip.

Once I accomplished this, I also crawled over to the car's side door. Keeping low and admonishing us to do the same, Jeeves slid into the car and behind the wheel. Holly and I quickly followed, keeping below the top of the dashboard. A split second after I closed the door Jeeves gunned the engine and we were throwing gravel on headless Bob.

None of us spoke for several minutes. You could see the silence in our faces. And I couldn't help thinking how different this was from our earlier leisurely three hour drive. . .could this be the same day? I was reminded of something Sherlock Holmes creator Sir Arthur Conan Doyle had once said, "Life is infinitely stranger than anything which the mind of men could invent." Maybe we had slipped into some parallel universe hell. You can never tell.

The silence was finally broken by Holly. Looking straight ahead and speaking in almost a whisper she asked, "Where are we going?" When no answer was forthcoming she repeated her question, "Where are we going?" Tears slid down cheeks still red with Bob's dried blood.

Our man Jeeves finally answered, with no hint of the bored stuffiness he had displayed earlier, "I'm taking you back to Mr. Schickel's. He told me if anything unusual happened, we were to come straight back."

Giving Holly a gentle hug I said, "Well, I'd say we are more than qualified for that 'unusual' tag line." She gave me a modest smile and cried on my shoulder. As I made with fatherly small talk to Holly, Jeeves reported to Schickel by cell phone.

In what seemed like no time at all Jeeves was turning into Schickel's farmyard. Like a worried parent on prom night, James was visible sitting at a downstairs window as we rolled into the parking area. And he was up and coming down the walk before we were hardly out of the limo.

With obvious concern over what had happened, he rushed to us, zeroing in on Holly. "My dear, I'm so sorry this had to happen. Life is not supposed to work this way. This is the kind of thing that drove me to be alone with my movies."

Holly gave him a little smile and said, "I'm okay now." But it was not a convincing "reading." Though Schickel meant well, this sent Holly into the tear mode once again.

Giving her shoulder a light squeeze, he said, "As much as it's in my power, I promise we'll get through this."

Turning to me (Jeeves had already disappeared into the house), Schickel added, "And I make the same pledge to you, Dr. Caine."

"Just call me David," I said.

"David it is," he answered.

Comforted by his grandfatherly take-charge manner and still a bit numb, I asked, "What should we do now?"

"Well, first why don't we go into the house and give you two a chance to clean up. I've already laid out towels and robes and what not in the guest rooms. Just follow me."

So that's how Holly and I came to spend the night at this reclusive film collector's house. True to his word, everything was ready for us in his four star guest suites, with more framed original full-sheet movie posters and lobby cards everywhere, not to mention two tiled shower facilities big enough to be showcased in *Citizen Kane*. As an exercise to keep my mind off of how the midget's head had turned into a substance resembling *so much* guacamole, I decided to pay extra attention to every cinematic detail of Schickel's museum-like home. An additional coping aid was the fact that Bob had essentially been a little turd.

As was consistent with other parts of the house, the movie memorabilia matched the settings. The bath and shower areas had a series of original Esther Williams movie posters. She's the one-time swimming star now famous for her water ballet films of the 1940s. The cinema art in the guest bedrooms included original posters from Woody Allen's *Sleeper*, Disney's *Sleeping Beauty*, and two titles appropriately macabre given the killing of Bob — *The Sleeping Car Murder* (a French classic about a mad killer) and Bogie's celebrated film noir caper *The Big Sleep*. Nice touch. I don't know about Holly, but I was feeling better already.

About the same time Holly and I had cleaned up and finished exploring, the delightful smell of bacon and eggs found its way into our dressing areas. Joining Schickel for a second time in his kitchen, he had two place settings ready for us. "I hope you two like bacon and eggs. I've got some red wine on the sideboard there, too. I'm afraid I was watching *Monsieur Verdoux* when you called, and this was what Chaplin was fixing for an unexpected guest in that picture."

For a fellow who had been so quiet the first time around, Schickel was now oozing innate decency. Holly and I each went through two helpings of his bacon and eggs; and he even pulled out the cold cuts from earlier in the day.

When we stopped eating everything that wasn't nailed down, I asked Schickel if we should call the police.

"What would be the point?" he answered defensively. "We'd have to spill Evert's little game, and maybe be booked for withholding evidence. Plus, there are people who'd be all too happy to somehow implicate you in Pee Wee Bob's death. Surely you've been through enough."

My halting response was, "I grant you there's enough Freudian material there to reupholster 600 therapy couches, but I hated leaving him by the side of the road."

A harshness seemed to come over Schickel's face and he said in evenly measured words, "David, I doubt you've ever taken a stupid breath — don't start now." He paused at this point to cut some pumpernickel bread with a knife the size of a horse's leg. It was a dramatic accent to what he'd just said. But as if to underline it he added, "Do you follow my drift?"

"In technicolor," I answered.

His change in tone had put a chill in the air and his later attempts at more jovial banter seemed forced. But Schickel did share, maybe to garner brownie points, that he had read through Mildred's script pages without cracking any hidden code Evert might have added. Schickel's theory, however, was that *Charlie Chaplin and the Time*

Machine was close at hand. "Evert talked about it enough that I sensed it was under the same roof. . .like he was screening it nightly."

Still put off by Schickel's momentary revealing of a dark side (preferring, as I do, a more genial form of dementia), I feigned tiredness after a few more minutes and retired to my guest room, with Holly going on to hers. But she joined me in my suite shortly thereafter.

"What do you make of Schickel?" she asked. "Do you really think he's as much in the dark about all this as we are?"

"Yeah, for some reason I do. He sort of reminds me of something Evert used to say, 'I don't want this for money, chalk, or marbles.'"

"Is there more to that, or am I supposed to guess?"

"They're both into playing games. It's no wonder Schickel signed on to Evert's little after life scavenger hunt."

At this point we were startled by a knock at the door. In fact, Holly, who was sitting on the end of the bed, somehow went straight up, with a hang time to rival Michael Jordan. The degree of difficulty in Olympic terms was at least a 9.5. With regard to me, I just let out a little gasp, like something cold had touched my neck. But I'm sure my peepers briefly assumed that bug-eyed state so common in old horror films.

When Holly stopped being an astronaut she managed to squeak out a timid, "Yes?"

"It's me — Schickel," came the quick reply. "Can I come in?"

"It's your house," I said.

Schickel rushed in like a kid at Christmas. "Take a look at this!" he fairly shouted. He was waving Mildred's script pages as if he'd hit the lottery. "Pee Wee did us a favor bleeding all over this. Checkout these words — the first letter in each one."

He laid four separate pages out on an end table. Several letters were circled, with each one "bleeding" ink which had seemingly been applied more recently. That is, someone — possibly Evert — had typed over these specific letters to accent them. Unfortunately, it hadn't proven that distinctive. . .until the blood drew attention to the tampering by making this more recent inking run.

"You get it?" asked an excited Schickel.

"Yeah," I said, though my response was far from convincing.

"You don't look like you get it," he responded.

Coming to my rescue Holly interjected, "We get it. The circled letters represent a code word. So what's the magic term or terms?"

The letters spelled c-a-t-a-c-o-m-b. "What the hell does that mean?" asked a suddenly frustrated Schickel. "Did he plant the Charlie film among some ancient stiffs?"

"Not necessarily," I answered with a chuckle. "The term 'catacomb' is also the local nickname for the passageways under our campus."

"Underground passages?" asked Schickel. "Whatever for?"

"Well, there are a raft of reasons," I said, "From storage to easy access to the various heating and cooling systems around the university."

"Storage?" he repeated, suddenly quite interested in my university chronicle.

"Yeah," I explained, "both the library and the art gallery maintain temperature controlled storage facilities down there."

"Could Evert have had access to any of this?" Schickel asked.

"It's possible," I replied. "He was in pretty tight with Dr. Ford, who runs the Special Collections Department in the university library. Regardless, it's my understanding that security down there isn't exactly Ft. Knox. But I've never had a reason to check it out."

"Until now," offered Holly.

"Well put my dear," said Schickel, as a broad smile enveloped his face. Addressing me he asked, "David, would it be possible for you to do a little catacomb exploring, once you got back to school?"

"I think that might be arranged but it could be the proverbial needle in a haystack . . . ."

"You never can tell," said Holly. "While there's probably a lot down there, Evert might have been relatively up front about marking the film can for *Charlie Chaplin and the Time Machine* — figuring no one but us would be looking in the 'catacombs.'"

"Holly might have something," I said. If it's down there, an obvious marking might have been Evert's contingency plan, on the off chance we hadn't broken this latest code."

"Could you run that by me again?" asked a puzzled looking Schickel, who was scratching his head like humorist Will Rogers when the plot wasn't going smoothly.

"Sure," I said. "Anytime you hide something there's always the risk that whoever you intended it for *won't* decipher your clues. But instead of it then being lost forever, a long term climate controlled storage area safeguards said object indefinitely. And if obviously tagged, the university connection almost guarantees that its eventual discoverer would be sympathetic to its significance."

"Well, I think you took the long way around the barn with that explanation," Schickel said. "But your theory makes sense. I'd wondered myself what would happen to the film if you didn't find it."

"I hate to break up this party," yawned Holly, "but I need to crash. I'm ready for the sound sleep of the stupid."

"Yes, of course," smiled Schickel. Turning his gaze from her to me he asked, "What time do you want to be taken back in the morning?"

"As early as possible," I answered. "Would seven work?"

"Certainly," said Schickel.

"One more thing," I asked. "Could we trouble you for some loaner duds in the morning. Our other stuff is no longer serviceable."

"I'm already on top of it," he said. "Each of your closets has several things to choose from — help yourself. So, if there's nothing else, I'll let you turn in. Good night."

Once he had left Holly apologized, "I'm sorry to be so tired. It seems like my bod has thrown a rod. First, I was a zombie after the shooting, followed by all my waterworks —"

"Forget it kiddo, I'm a guy that can cry, too. True, it's usually after I've hurt myself . . . ."

Holly laughed and threw a pillow at my head. It was an upbeat close to a less than upbeat day.

Though I tucked Holly into Evert's other guest bedroom that night, the following morning I found her asleep at the foot of my bed. Otherwise, it was an uneventful exit from Schickel's place that morning, though he laid a parting caveat on us: "We might be through with the past but the past isn't necessarily through with us — so be careful."

He also gave me his number so I could be in touch, once I'd tapped into the university's "catacombs." Then we were gone. Holly slept most of the three hour drive back, while I rehashed the whole Evert/Chaplin puzzle in my mind. I felt like that Aerosmith lyric about "tap dancing on a land mine." At home there was a message on my machine from Ms. Hopper. Tomorrow was Friday and she didn't want me to forget our little get-together.

Chapter 11

*Visitors. . .greeted him [Chaplin] like a god on furlough
from Olympus*
        — the comedian's son Michael (1966).

In the morning Holly decided to sleep in, so I went to school by myself. I was lecturing on science fiction and fantasy in the genre class, but the film noir elements of the previous evening wouldn't leave my head. I listened to the news on the car radio, but there was zero about a Munchkin with an exploding head.

At school I checked my e-mail and phone messages, with nothing of any importance turning up, though Ms. Hopper had left yet another reminder about that night. I glanced at the framed letters over my computer. In this age of impersonal electronic communication, I cling to letters. Like photos, they're pieces of time, something you can touch and re-read long after the correspondent has left your life.

This was yet another way in which Evert and I connected. In fact, while I hadn't thought about it until just then, the old professor's love of letters might have helped fuel this mystery he'd gotten Holly and me involved in. In a way, he had been corresponding from the grave, what with his witty notes each step of the way. Plus, Evert had even thrown in historical correspondence when he gifted us with those letters from what might be called the "Chaplin women."

Evert had always kidded me about swiping the framed letter I had from Alec Guinness, one of the few prominent performers he had never met. We were both huge fans of the Ealing Studio dark comedies which often starred Guinness in the late 1940s and early 1950s, such as *Kind Hearts and Coronets*, *The Lavender Hill Mob*, and *The Ladykillers*. Fittingly, I had met Guinness after a dark comedy London stage production of *A Walk in the Woods*, while I was in England doing research on a book about Ealing.

Anyway, I scored a couple of interview lunch dates with Guinness, and he was more than helpful with the book. Indeed, he'd even written me some follow-up thoughts after I'd gone home. Besides sharing his comedy insights, he'd given me major credibility with my then young daughters, more than any of my published books ever had — "Obiwan Kenobi is writing to you, Daddy? Why? Does he talk about Luke? Are you going to be in a *Star Wars* movie? What do you mean his real name isn't Obiwan Kenobi? Have you always known that? . . ." Thus, framing one of his letters worked on several levels for me, from documenting that I knew a real Jedi knight, to a time capsule of memories about my daughters as little people. And now I could add thoughts of Evert to that list.

Leave it to Mark to bring me out of my poignant time tripping with a little bawdy humor. He'd just come by my office and stuck his head in the door.

"Sci fi and fantasy this week, right?! [There was a syllabus on the door.] I've got the perfect limerick for you:

'There was a young spaceman named Joe
Who was making a spacegirl too slow.
She said, Don't be morbid:
Eject into orbit,
Because all my systems are GO!' "

Laughing, I said, "You're thinking too much."

"I seriously doubt that," he replied. And he was gone. Of course, "In and out quickly" was one of his mottoes, with the purely Mark disclaimer — "Proven to be effective in the bedroom."

As I glanced at my watch I realized that this time Mark might have dashed by from pure lateness. It was the top of the hour, and then some. So I made like Jesse Owens and raced to my 10 o'clock.

It was a full house today in class — about 40 pleasantly rowdy students. Most of them were shooting the shit with whomever was sitting nearby; a few kids were hidden behind newspapers, and two or three were stuffing their faces with vending machine mystery food. (The break room should sell insurance, like at the airport.) Then I received a major league shock. Among that moving myriad of distracted faces, one kisser was looking *dead on* at me — Ms. Hopper. I was reminded of the scene from Hitchcock's *Strangers on a Train*. The picture's nominal star, Farley Granger, is a tennis player in the midst of a major match. The heads of the audience turn rhythmically back and forth, following the batted ball — except for Robert Walker's psychopath. There to trade murders, his eyes always stare straight ahead at Granger.

As I glanced around the room for objects I might dive behind in case she was packin' a rod, my mind went into overdrive for other explanations about why she might be there. Maybe she was just a few credits shy of a degree in criminal justice. Maybe the cable reception had gone out in her hotel room and she had come hoping I'd be showing film clips. Maybe she just wondered how many college males she could arouse, not to mention those two dykes in the corner. As it was, people were already starting to check her out, given that, as Dashiell Hammett might have described Ms. Hopper — "her thin black dress of cotton material clung to her with an effect of dampness."

Given that I was still alive, however, I decided she was merely on reconnaissance for our "date," and I best start class. Things had quieted down somewhat when I walked in but it wasn't like Patton had just gotten out of his jeep or anything. Nor do I even try to command stereotypical academic respect, à la John Houseman's neo-Nazi professor in *The Paper Chase*. That's lucky for my students, since every so often there's one or two who deserve to be butt-kicked to Kalamazoo. For example, rarely does a term go by without some kid asking, after an absence, "Did I miss anything important?" After curbing the desire to go right for his eyes, I always want to reply, "Nothing you would have understood." But I don't. Life's too short to have a hissy-fit over every little thing. My philosophy: "The situation is definitely hopeless but not serious."

Along those lines, I like to start each class with a little humor. Sadly, this often involves questions about previous lectures, but that's the nature of the beast. This session was no different. One of my front row regulars, a shapely coed named Rita, with the vacuous blonde good looks of a young Cameron Diaz, asked me to once again differentiate between realism and formalism. I should add, it took me a moment to respond. Lovely Rita (sorry, Beatles reflex) evidently had just had, you should pardon the expression, a stud put in her mouth, or, more precisely — her tongue. So Rita's question sounded like one long vowel moment — which was reminiscent of Walter Brennan's dialogue in *Red River* after he lost his false teeth in a poker game.

Of course, Rita's speech pattern was a damn sight more sexy, given that since she was not yet used to her stud. As she spoke, her tongue playfully flitted out — raking the silver ball of the stud that pierced it across her teeth — an oral xylophone. As Warner Bros' amorous skunk, Pepe LePew, might have described it — "ze music of love, no?" Had Rita been so inclined (reclined?), and her football star boyfriend had opted for the priesthood (or been hit by a Mack truck), every guy in the room would have been ready for. . .well, you know.

I kept my realism versus formalism response short. The former keyed upon content, I said, while the latter focused on style. Thus, any time a director called attention to himself by way of technique (such as razzle-dazzle editing, slow motion, freeze frames, etc.), you're talking formalism. In contrast, when using long takes and long shots, as in a classic John Ford Western — basic realism is coming at you.

Through all this explanation Ms. Hopper sat in rapt attention, like I was on the verge of calling out a winning lottery number. I half expected her to pull a notebook out of her handbag and start scribbling away. So for her benefit I added, "You can also determine whether you're more inclined towards realism or formalism by where you sit in a theatre. If you plant yourself close to the screen and like to get lost in the image — you're a realist. If you prefer to sit further away in order to be forever aware of the boundaries of screen, you're a formalist. Personally, I like to sit in the front row. My second wife, however, preferred being way, way back — like Chicago. So [pause] I divorced her."

As in past semesters, this got a big laugh. But this time it also produced a question — from Ms. Hopper. "Where did your first wife like to sit?"

"She was an Amish girl from Cedar Rapids," I said. "She couldn't see movies. So we usually just stayed home and watched cable."

I received another good response, and a modest smile from Evert's niece, with a soft spoken, "Good to know."

I moved on to my lecture, but my mind was a million miles away. Why the hell was she here? I figured I'd get some answers after class. Instead she threw me a curve. At one point during my riveting discourse on sci fi and fantasy I briefly turned to put a few terms on the board. When I again faced the class Ms. Hopper had disappeared. However, she left a provocative calling card. After class a student who had been seated near her handed me a large manila envelope. "The woman in the tight dress gave me a twenty spot to give you this."

Someone, presumably Evert's niece, had scribbled across the outside of the envelope — "Here's another side to your hero." Inside was a lengthy letter on brittle yellowing stationery with many of the handwritten words smudged, as if from tears. Simply dated 1921, the correspondence was to Mildred, and was signed with an elaborate capital C. Oh my God, this had to be Chaplin. I quickly looked around me, in order to see if either Ms. Hopper or any archival police were watching me. With no apparent surveillance going on, I hurried off to the privacy of my office to read the letter. I soon was engrossed:

Dear Mildred,

I don't write letters. If I'm going to pick up a pen I want to do something creative. This is my second letter to you. That means you are now two letters up on my dear brother Sydney. I don't plan to write again.

The Jesus film will not be released — not now, not ever. It was an interesting experiment, but an experiment just the same. America is not ready for such a picture, nor will it ever be.

Today one has to have more than curly hair above his shoulders. You've got to know your onions. I know movies. I am currently working on another experimental project — a script tentatively called *A Woman of France*. At the moment I am at an impasse. I'm chopping away, but no chips are flying.

Still, I'm fascinated by the subject matter — a sophisticated comedy of manners. I don't think it's a commercial property. And I won't cheat by putting myself in it. But the film might speak to the artistic community. I will even go out on a limb and suggest the critics might like it.

Then again, this experiment might never see the light of day either. The *Charlie Chaplin Dog and Pony Show* is all avant-garde stuff looking for a mainstream audience. I don't expect you to understand this. I could never reach your mind, cluttered as it is with pink-ribboned foolishness.

While I had no need to marry an encyclopedia, we often seemed in two worlds. Even now you ask me to release a movie that could keep me from making other movies. Kierkegaard once wrote that if Christ were to return "he would perhaps not be put to death but would be ridiculed. This is martyrdom in the age of reason." At this time my Jesus picture would open me up to ridicule, too. It's a pity, since my interpretation of Him is refreshingly upbeat, rather than that sad-eyed, pious character in the storybooks. I'm disappointed enough, so you don't need to burn three feet off my tail every time you're unhappy.

Ironically, while I've always been fascinated by the character of Christ, I have little time for Christianity, the last resort for desperate people. To paraphrase that Ring Lardner baseball crack currently making the rounds, "They call it left field, because they fill all the other places first and then if there's any one left they send him out there." People play lots of positions in life, but Christianity's calculated ability to make human beings unhappy ultimately puts most folks in a repentant left field. Kierkegaard was on to something when he said Christianity was the invention of the devil.

When I first came to Hollywood all I wanted to do was save enough money to buy a chicken farm. I have raised my goals. You should do the same.

Forget the Jesus picture. There are no other places for appeal. So stop harassing me and my friends. You received a handsome divorce settlement, plus a healthy bonus for the experiment. Remember, besides my controlling interest in United Artists, I have influence at all the major studios. If you want to continue your career, such as it is, you'll retire from your Jesus Crusade.

Good-bye forever, C

Well, while I could see how Chuck's hardball letter would not have endeared him to Ms. Hopper, his take on the Christ picture made perfect sense. To put it in a punning perspective, the press would have crucified him. I didn't know where this left me on the evening date with Evert's niece. But by giving me a letter with Chaplin's frank discussion of the Jesus film, she was saying I know you know more than you're admitting.

I had another class, after which I cancelled my office hours and went home. Holly was still sawing logs, so I made a few calls and then started to fix us something to eat. The aroma of bacon and cheese omelets had her in the kitchen quicker than those cartoon characters that float along upon the fragrance of their favorite food.

I got her up to speed on the events of the morning, including my sexy auditor.

"You're kidding. The one time I miss class—"

"Yeah, right."

"You know what I mean. Hey, let me see the letter."

I carefully took the fragile pages out of my leather satchel and handed them to her as if they were the original documents comprising the Magna Carta. Of course, in my Chaplin forever household they were *more* valuable. Holly slowly read through the letter and let out a whistle.

"Do you have to give this back?"

"I'm hoping not, but we'll see."

"Are you still planning to meet her tonight?"

"Why not?"

"Oh, you know, Dad. Let's add this up, things like fucking exploding heads, killer Buicks, heads crushed by famous movie birds . . . . Maybe if you wore a suit of armor tonight I'd feel better. You know, Raymond Chandler used to call film noir types 'tarnished knights.'"

"It's just not being done socially this season."

"Yeah, well I grieve over all these piss-elegant rules late at night when I can't sleep."

"When's the last time you had trouble with the sandman, Sleeping Beauty?"

"Okay, okay. Just be careful, Pop. I really think she's behind all this. But who knows, maybe meeting with her will help us crack this."

"Don't worry about me. I'm just anxious to put our adventure in fast-forward before everyone, including Santa Claus at the North Pole, knows what we're about."

We finished eating without saying much more. Shortly thereafter I drove her back to the dorm and then returned to the apartment. I resumed working on my current book project, a biography of screwball comedy actress Carole Lombard — the "Profane Angel." The moniker came from the fact that she was a heavenly beauty, yet swore like the proverbial sailor. Legend has it that Lombard once told future husband Clark Gable that she was "half saint and half whore." He replied, "Here's hoping I get the half that eats."

Anyway, writing is my panacea for stress, or just about anything. And I had never been in more need of a distraction. Evert's bludgeoning death, the Munchkin's exploding head, a murderous Buick. . .all these things made me feel like a broken end of the film flapping round and round while the projectionist is off in the john, unaware of the breakage. I was reminded of novelist J. Anthony Lukas' observation, "All writers are to some extent damaged. [Why, thank you, Mr. Lukas.] Writing is our way of repairing ourselves." I think there is a lot of truth to that, though in Lukas' case the repair part didn't quite take. He later committed suicide. Of course, as the time approached for me to get ready for my meeting with Ms. Hopper, suicide was the least of my worries — with regard to how I might buy the farm.

Chapter 12

Nothing is permanent in this wicked world. Not even our troubles.

> —*Chaplin rationalizing over his next murder as the title character of* Monsieur Verdoux *(1947).*

I showered and shaved; the phrase "five o'clock shadow" might have been coined with me in mind. I put on a pale blue dress shirt and some new tan slacks. The hotel was only a fifteen-minute drive from my apartment, but I left early to get the lay of the land. The plan was to play dumb, which as Holly might have cracked, "Shouldn't be much of a stretch." I would continue to stonewall over knowing *anything* about a lost Chaplin film. Plus, I would do my best to find out what Ms. Hopper knew about said movie and/or the death of the midget.

The Rivera Hotel was a landmark in Middletown. The twenty-story structure was in the heart of the downtown. Recently remodeled, it boasted a number of penthouse suites named after prominent Indiana-born entertainers. As luck would have it, Ms. Hopper was staying in the Carole Lombard suite. After getting her number from a goofy-looking desk clerk, sort of a live action Yosemite Sam, the express elevator had me on the twentieth floor in a millisecond, though several of my organs felt like they were still taking the stairs. Hopefully, they would be up by the time I needed them.

Ms. Hopper's suite was just to my right as I got off the elevator. There was a beautifully framed Lombard lobby card, from the picture *Supernatural*, next to the door. Little did I know at the time how appropriate this bit of decorative art would be.

The door was open about six inches; evidently Yosemite had called to announce my arrival. I knocked gently and said, "Ms. Hopper?"

"Come in, please."

I entered an elegant living room area done in silver and gray, Lombard's favorite color combination. The furniture was French Provincial, with a wraparound sofa in front of the fireplace. The bricks were of a lighter gray hue than the rest of the room, and there was a large triple-matted photo of Lombard and Clark Gable above the hearth. The dark, almost black, mahogany frame matched the one in the hallway.

The lovely setting, however, had yet to produce a hostess. Then, like a ghost, Ms. Hopper was suddenly beside me. Her seemingly nether world arrival was complimented by a filmy, semi-transparent, negligee-like gown that left very little to the imagination. The fuck-me red lips were now of a subdued hue, like she was trying to match the room's bloodless color scheme, but the x-rated message was the same.

"Professor, I'm so happy you could make it. I was afraid my hasty exit today would scare you off."

"Well, Ms. Hopper —"

"Please, call me Lola."

"Alright. That was quite the letter you left me."

"Won't you sit down." She motioned me towards the sofa, and then joined me there. "Yes, I thought the letter might better explain my distaste for Chaplin, as well as prove to you that there was a Jesus movie."

"I was shocked." I only hoped my nose wasn't growing as I said it. "There's not even a hint of any such film in the Chaplin literature."

"Hopefully, it opened your eyes to his cruelness, too." Her lovely high-cheekboned face tightened as she said this.

"Well, his cavalier tendencies are not exactly news. But I grant you he treated Mildred meanly, though his position on this bombshell of a movie I understand."

Lola's hands clenched into elegant fists as her rising voice screeched, "Is this more academic elitism?"

"I don't know, is this some sort of B-movie seduction scene?" As I made a motion to get up, she slid closer and lightly put a hand on my shoulder.

In a softer tone she almost purred, "Please, let's not argue again. Have you ever felt like a wasted life?"

"Only when I'm awake."

Smiling now, she replied, "I'm pretty much an open book. Actually, compared to all the letters behind your name, I'm more of an open pamphlet. And the pamphlet says, 'Get that film, whatever it takes.'" She then snuggled closer and brought her lips slowly and tentatively towards mine, before giving me an open-mouthed kiss.

While hardly a convincing performance, it had been eons since anything remotely this sexy had occurred to me. So I joined in. After all, I could relate to that legendary anonymous antihero who once observed, "The last woman I was in was the Statue of Liberty."

Soon we were into your basic "caressing and groping 101." This was followed by helping each other out of our clothing. But you surely know that drill. Lola decided, however, we should only partly undress. Her theory was that it'd be more exciting that way, like the high school quickie in the backseat of someone's car. It worked for me.

Only Lola didn't treat it like a quickie. She had a wonderful way of rubbing her breasts over what Robin Williams likes to call "the pulsating python of love." Yes, it showed a nice spirit on her part. Of course, when her face went further south I had to immediately go into my think baseball scenario, or our film noir icebreaker would have ended way too early.

As we eventually intertwined, skin to skin, the sexual heat factor reminded me, paradoxically, of an old romantic axiom: "It was as if I'd been taken with a new pleasurable form of fever." Okay, so I briefly succumbed to a woman using her body for a loveless, godless goal — to join the bad guys. Jeez, cut me some slack. This is a standard plot development for film noir. It's in all the handbooks: "The detective, or quasi-detective protagonist [that would be me] is required at some point to become amorously involved with the bitch goddess femme fatale [pencil in Lola]." But don't take my word for it. As Casey Stengel used to say, "You can look it up." Anyway, several overwritten pulp fiction sex quotes from my horny teenage reading came to mind, like "her downy-matted sanctuary," or biting flanks and nipples which would "bleed pure butterscotch."

Still, this was a dicey spot for me. After the bitch goddess gives it her best sexual shot the noir male goes one of two paths. He can become a pussy-whipped tool of the femme fatale, á la Fred MacMurray in *Double Indemnity*. Or, the tough guy detective type can get some ballast in his britches and have the sexy but evil skirt take the fall, such as Bogart sending Mary Astor upriver in *The Maltese Falcon*.

Now, just between you and me and a film noir fencepost, who do you think I'm more likely to emulate. Will it be the American Film Institute's pick as the coolest star of the twentieth century (Bogart, with apologies to James Dean), or that *My Three Sons* guy with the bad toupee (MacMurray)? Good, I'm glad we understand each other. Personally, I feel my brief dalliance with Lola need not even be defended on film noir lines. It was simply a fundamental fact of life. As Woody Allen once observed, "Sex without love may be an empty experience, but as empty experiences go, it's one of the best."

The only time it got weird with Lola was *after* the sex. We lay there half asleep for a while and then she gently but firmly pulled me to my feet and led me by the hand to a portion of the wall just opposite the fireplace. The space she zeroed in on contained an all but invisible door to the bedroom.

I was totally impressed. I'd only seen that kind of thing in the movies. This imperceptible door explained how she had so suddenly just appeared at my side earlier in the evening. Okay, while she entered the other room to, I assume, go to bed, I started playing with the door. I was like a kid at Christmas with a new toy. I closed the door and felt along the opening. I made like a spy tapping on the wall for a hidden mechanism. I then started checking out the other walls. Maybe there was a video arcade, or a bowling alley. After all, this was a penthouse suite. Lombard loved horses, well not like Catharine the Great, but she did enjoy traditional riding. Maybe there was a hidden stable door nearby. Then I was thinking, screw the stables, I'm starved. I'll look for an indiscernible door to the kitchen, or maybe one that just opened directly into one of those little hotel bars. Yeah, I felt like an $10 beer.

Unfortunately, the only quasi-invisible opening I managed to find was the connecting door that lead to the next suite. But unlike most hotels, where it was a shared door, these suites each had their own, separated by a cave-like hall of about six feet. The design seemed like wasted space, but architects just don't have me check their blueprints like they used to. Regardless, there wasn't an $10 beer in sight.

About this time Lola came out in this sort of Merlin the Magician outfit, with matching threads for me. I wasn't really into this Arthurian unisex look, but it's not like we were throwing a slumber party, so I played along. I figured we'd have sex in the bedroom, and then I'd sleep the sleep of an overage Walter Mitty.

But when she opened the door this time it was like midnight mass at St. Patrick's Cathedral. There must have been a million candles burning around an altar. I thought, great. It was bad enough I couldn't find the kitchen; now I had to go to communion. However, when I looked closer at this makeshift altar I realized the headliner was not the late great Jesus, but rather Lola's grandmother — Mildred Harris. I had stumbled into séance city. Lola was a black magic medium, ready to play some sort of spiritualist spin the bottle.

Still holding my hand, Lola led me to a small round table and chairs near the Harris altar. As we sat down she explained, "As a spiritualist I am in direct communication with my grandmother. I wanted to tell you sooner, but I was afraid you wouldn't understand."

"Yeah, I bet you get a lot of that."

Smiling without separating her lips, Lola answered, "It's a lot to digest. But after our little *dance* [Lola nodded towards the living room], I'm willing to show you my hand. Do you believe in love at first sight?"

"Only when I've been drinking."

She shrugged, "Not even a little?"

"Well, it would be a great time saver; I'll give you that."

"I've been attracted to you since Evert's funeral. But I don't leave things to chance. I also dabble in astrology and numerology—"

"Imagine that," I said.

Ignoring this crack, she continued, "Doing my homework, I found that everything about you, from the alignment of the planets when you were born, to the number of letters in your full name, suggested we were a match."

"Darn, and I thought it was just my great personality. I'm pleased that you're pleased, but I don't know where that leaves us."

Placing her hands on her hips, she said, "One woman can make a difference."

"It would have to be a really big woman," I replied. "Caines marry for better or worse, but it's usually the latter."

"Will you join me in contacting my grandmother? She can be quite convincing."

"I don't know; have you got FCC clearance? Is it safe? I heard once that folks who hang out with the dead are sometimes called 'missing persons.'"

Lola scowled. "Enough with the jokes. It's really quite easy. I merely place my grandmother's ring [which she produced from a pocket in her Merlin getup] on my finger and concentrate on the altar pictures while chanting her name. Within a few moments the channeling begins."

I wanted to ask if she needed a remote for that, but I thought better of it. Instead, I said, "Okay, I guess. When in Rome . . . ."

"Excellent. Now, before we start you need to have some questions—"

"Boy, have I got questions."

Lola's scary scowl returned, which was not unlike the look of Judith Anderson's chilling housekeeper in *Rebecca*. Lola continued, "You need to have questions for Mildred. Besides the whereabouts of the Jesus film, ask whatever. I just want you to believe in this. Oh, and she might get on her soapbox and ignore everything."

"How long does one of these visits last?"

"No more than ten or fifteen minutes. They're very intense, and yet I remember very little. I am depending on you, Professor, for feedback. Shall we begin?"

I nodded. Lola put on the ring and quickly went into a trance state which would not have looked out of place in Val Lewton's *I Walked With a Zombie*. Her high-cheekboned beauty slowly became disturbingly skull-like. Her breathing was labored. Beads of sweat appeared on her forehead. There was a sudden coldness to the room. I felt like an antiheroic Bob Hope exploring a haunted house in *Ghost Breakers*. And I wasn't prepared for the voice change — Mildred's voice.

"I am here," said Lola as her grandmother. The sound was a low throaty whisper, not unlike a bad impersonation of Marilyn Monroe. Though it came out of Lola's mouth, there was little movement of her lips. It was like a ventriloquist act from hell, or maybe the road company of *Beetlejuice*.

Not knowing what to say, I blurted out, "What was marriage to Chaplin like?"

A storm cloud came over Lola's face. Tears started streaming down her cheeks. Soon my medium was shaking with sobs. Jeez, how do you comfort a dead soul? I should call up my third wife. No, that would be even scarier. I went with another question.

In as comforting a voice as possible I asked, "What was it like playing Mary Magdalene?" The sobs immediately stopped, and Lola's countenance became childlike. A giggle escaped from her lips.

"What's so funny?"

Mildred replied, "Charlie always acted out everyone's part. He was a funny Mary — skipping with Jesus. And when he would play both parts at once [another giggle], it was hard to breathe. As Christ, he would also forgive people during breaks in the shooting."

"Do you know where the film is now?"

Lola's face assumed that overly quizzical expression common to brainstorming silent screen heroines — two parts Mary Pickford, with a dash of Lillian Gish. Speaking slowly, this little voice said, "It is somewhere underground, far from Hollywood."

Great, that narrows it down. Note to self: when packing for the next world, tuck in an address book. Lola's kisser was starting to look really strained, so I figured one more question — "Is your granddaughter a threat to me?"

"G-E-T O-U-T! G-E-T O-U-T! G-E-T O-U-T!" screeched Mildred's voice. I damn near soiled myself. What made it even worse was the speech inflection — like that scary pod-person noise at the close of the second *Invasion of the Body Snatchers*.

My first response was to — G-E-T O-U-T! But if Lola was dependent upon me to fill her in, I was ahead of the game. I would just tell her what was most expedient. I wouldn't really have to lie about the whereabouts of the Jesus film, because Mildred, bless her heart, hadn't exactly given me the best directions.

I was soon thankful I stuck around for another reason. As Lola slowly came out of her séance state, a condition not unlike whiskey coma, she had several hallucinations. One involved our favorite Munchkin, Bob, with the special effects head. While I couldn't follow all of Lola's babbling, it seemed clear that she had ordered the hit.

More importantly to me, however, was Lola's Charlie Chaplin hallucination. It gave me an idea for some spiritualistic sneakiness, if I could elicit the help of Holly and my oversexed colleague, Mark. But I'm getting ahead of myself. Regardless, at this point Lola's eyes were wide open, yet she was in the midst of a five-minute conversation with Chaplin! Unfortunately, I was not privy to his portion of the dialogue. But there were actual pauses in her speech, when she seemed to be listening to another voice. I kept expecting to suddenly hear *The Twilight Zone* music, with Rod Serling sauntering out and doing his signature opening:

There is a fifth dimension beyond that which is known to man. It is a dimension as vast as space and as timeless as infinity. It is the middle ground between light and shadow, between science and superstition, and it lies between the pit of man's fears and the summit of his knowledge. This is the dimension of his imagination. It is an area we call "The Twilight Zone."

"Professor Caine—"

"Rod?" I answered, as I came out of my "trance." Lola had returned to the living while I was having my own hallucination!

"Is everything all right, Professor? What did Mildred say?" Lola had gone from comatose mode to the metabolism of a cheerleader on diet pills.

With complete honesty I answered, "It was fascinating. She gave me a nice feel for the production of the Jesus film, which she really seemed to enjoy."

"But where is it now?" she practically shouted.

"Mildred didn't know, other than to say it wasn't in Hollywood. But what I want to hear about is *your* conversation with Chaplin."

"Huh? What are you talking about?"

"Listen with your eyes — look at me, Lola, and think. After Mildred's spirit left, you got into a spirited discussion with Chaplin. There didn't seem to be half the animosity I would have expected."

A flicker of recognition came to her eyes. "He was telling me something positive about Mildred, though I can't for the life of me remember what it was."

"I think we should visit with Mildred again, soon. And maybe you could tap back into your Chaplin conversation. How about tomorrow night?"

"No, I've got new associates — I'm booked. But how does Sunday night strike you?"

"Yeah, that would work. Shall we make it a date?"

"I think I'd like that," she answered in a seductive tone. "Just so long as we don't have to close the book on tonight."

So, as cover for the sake of a possible Sunday night plan, I was forced to bed her again. Work, work, work.

Chapter 13

I am beyond sleep to-night. . .I am in something new,
something pregnant with expectation. The immediate
future is too alluring for sleep.
    — Chaplin anticipating his 1921 return to Europe.

I slept very little after take two with Lola. My thoughts were on
Sunday night. I wanted to use Holly and Mark to stage a controlled
Chaplin hallucination. If I could soften Lola's perspective on the comedian, while convincing her I didn't have a clue about the mystery
film, maybe I could defuse the danger zone that *spirited* Mildred was
warning about. Jeez, I was already starting to sound like the *Psychic
Hotline*, or was that Johnny Carson's Carnac the Magnificent?

Of course, my biggest problem would be convincing Holly and
Mark that I wasn't off my nut. If they only could have been flies on
the wall last night. Well, not the whole time — just during the black
magic segment of the evening. Thus, when I start to explain this,
they'll probably think I've written one too many books about comedians. But come to think of it, there's a W. C. Fields story that fits my
plan perfectly. The frequently sauced Fields was once asked if he had
ever had DT's. The comedian replied, "I don't know. It's hard to tell
where Hollywood ends and the DT's begin." If my plan worked, it
would be hard to distinguish between Hollywood and a Holly hallucination.

At the earliest light I quietly got up and dressed. I scribbled a brief
message on a hotel note pad by the phone — "I'm looking forward to
Sunday night at 8." Normally, I don't like to steal away like that, but I
justified it on the grounds that she was probably a killer. Then, to borrow a phrase from my college students, I did "the walk of shame" out
to my car. Translation: after getting "lucky" some night, you're

forced to wear the same clothes back to your dorm the following morning.

At home I found Holly's shoes just inside the door. She must have come over last night to check on my Lola adventure. Sure enough, she was tucked in the guest bedroom, with a post-it note on the door — "Wake me when you come in." She had signed it — Dr. Watson. Smiling, I decided it was too early to get her up. In fact, I was suddenly nursing a tired headache and decided to crash myself.

The next thing I knew it was late morning and there was this heavenly smell of Belgian waffles coming from the kitchen. Shuffling out to the dining area I was spoofingly greeted by Chef Holly: "Well, if it isn't the legendary Don Juan, come home for his vitamins, no doubt."

"Guess what I've got?"

"Stumped the clinic again, Dad?"

"Don't be clever. I've just formulated the perfect plan. Of course, it involves dressing you up like Charlie Chaplin and acting ghost-like."

"Come again, Papa? Have you had another acid flashback?"

"No, but when I explain the evening I've just had, you'll think so. Ms. Hopper, or I should say Lola —"

"Go, Dad! I thought those were new notches on your belt."

Smiling, I continue, "Lola is a spiritualist, and last night she conjured up Mildred Harris."

"Wo, you're on the level? What's the old girl like?"

"Surprisingly sympathetic. She even warned me about Lola."

"Well, duh! A blind man with a cane could see she's bad news."

"Anyway, when Lola was coming out of her trance she had a seemingly positive Chaplin hallucination, all on her own. I think we can soften Lola's position even further if we stage a return visit by the *little fellow*. So *Charlie*, is your dance card free for some adventure Sunday night?"

"Sure, you know me. I'm a gypsy — born with rings in my ears." But then in a less flippant voice she asked, "You're sure about all this?"

"Absolutely. Lola is really open to suggestion as she comes out of the séance trance. If we can lower her intensity level on both Chuck and us, I think it will make her less dangerous."

"Wouldn't it be easier just to *chuck* her out the window?"

Laughing, I replied, "No, I think falling back on your comedy troupe skills would be our best bet. Just do the standard Charlie shtick you used for the Duck's Breath audition — shuffling gait, hat and cane acrobatics, the whole nine yards. Do you still have that costume?"

"Yeah, it's over at Mom's."

"Great, see if you can track it down today."

"Do I talk? How does my routine change her attitude?"

"That's where Mark comes in."

Suppressing a chuckle, Holly said, "Limerick Luke is going to be in on this, too? Forgive me if I don't think of him as the world's safest bet."

"Don't worry, his melodious pipes are just what we need for a VO of Chaplin from beyond the grave. Besides, Mark has a stake, of sorts, in this. Remember, he's the one that found Evert."

After our late Saturday breakfast, I dropped Holly at her mother's to look for the Charlie getup. As long as I was out, I then went by my office to see if I had any late afternoon messages from the previous day. There was nothing to phone home about, but Mark's office door, just down the hall from mine, was open.

Saving myself a call, I walked over and told him as much as he needed to know about the previous evening, as well as my plans for Sunday night.

"What if I was doing something that couldn't be cancelled?" he asked.

"When have you ever been doing anything that couldn't be cancelled?"

"True enough. I just didn't want you to think I was easy."

Unlike my semi-grounded daughter, Mark never batted an eye as I rehashed séance city with Lola. Moreover, he acted like my plan to stage a Charlie Chaplin hallucination for a spiritualist and suspected murderess was standard Sunday night fare. That being said, however, Mark was more than interested in the amorous side of the previous evening. I kept my comments here to a minimum, though he twice interrupted me with the tag line from his favorite *Saturday Night Live* sketch, "You da Lady's Man." Naturally, this was further milked with his hydraulic eyebrow action. Horniness notwithstanding, he had ideas, too.

"How about if I bring some Chaplin-composed music to our post-séance scam? It might enhance Holly's routine."

"Good idea. I'm partial to 'Smile' and 'This Is My Song' — which I have, if you need them."

"Should we all get together for a run through tomorrow?"

"You're reading my mind. How about my apartment, early afternoon? Oh, and I'm going to need you to book a penthouse suite at the Rivera. Don't worry; I'll reimburse you. Lola is in the Lombard. We need to be next door. If memory serves me, her suite is flanked by Red Skelton on one side, and Hoagy Carmichael on the other."

"Sounds like a celebrity roast, Hoosier style."

"That it does. Cross your fingers they're not booked. Being able to use an access door would simplify staging this thing. Well, I'm going to get out of here. *Thank you* for dong this; you're a real mensch. Call me if you think of anything else."

As I started to leave, Mark yelled, "David!" But before I could either respond or turn around, he again sang out — "You da Lady's Man!"

"The Lady's Man" went home to rest. I needed to get some thoughts down for Mark's VO, when Holly made like Chaplin's tramp. But I figured that could wait until morning. Instead, I got comfortable, poured myself a glass of wine, and picked out some favorite reading material.

My apartment has enough books to double as a lending library, so my selection was extensive. You know the way some women buy shoes — that's me and books. As a writer/scholar, to me books simply represent part of the territory. I also pepper them with margin notes and underlining, not to mention my own personalized index in the back of each book. I'm a demon for detail. All these voices make the craft of writing rather like consulting old friends — a joyful undertaking.

But on this night I didn't want enlightened assistance; I just wanted to be entertained. More specifically, I wanted to laugh and not think about Evert's violent Charlie mystery and that sexy psychopathic swami. So I turned to my favorite literary escape — a short story called "The Kugelmass Episode." I first came across it when my second marriage was unraveling. This guy Kugelmass was also an unhappily married professor. But his escape came in the form of a fantasy-like invention dreamed up by a scientist pal, that could transport him into the world of the written word. This enabled Kugelmass to make time with literature's most celebrated babes. He chose to have himself an affair with the title character from Flaubert's *Madame Bovary*.

As for my own Kugelmass fantasy mode, I would have preferred sexy Brett in Hemingway's *The Sun Also Rises*, or maybe Kurt Vonnegut's fictional film star Montana Wildhack from *Slaughterhouse Five*. Better yet, I'd have the transporting device converted so I could infiltrate the movies of my choice. I'd christen the machine the "*Si*nema Traveler." I'd be the one making time on the couch with Marilyn Monroe in *Some Like It Hot*. Or, maybe I'd go chasing after young Jane Fonda in the kinky outer space of *Barbarella* — a sexy take on the 41st century. Ah, so many provocative movies, so little time.

But true to my *antiheroic nature* (a.k.a. *we be fucked*), if I'd had access to such a machine I probably would have suffered the same comic nightmare that Kugelmass met. While attempting a sexy "trip" into *Portnoy's Complaint*, the transporter shorts out, the scientist/machine operator dies of a heart attack, and poor Kugelmass, instead of finding hot monkey lovin' in *Portnoy's Complaint*, turns up in an old textbook, *Remedial Spanish*, racing for his life from a spider-like irregular verb. I easily relate to a character who can't even get it right in his own fantasies. Given my background (four years of high school German — which I had arm wrestled to a draw), however, I probably would have been victimized by a Nazi noun.

After some Kugelmass comedy I felt better, though a half bottle of wine probably helped, too. (I have it from reliable sources that Sam Spade used to unwind with Abbott and Costello recordings and Dr. Pepper.) Regardless, I went to bed by midnight that night, an unbelievably early lights outs for me. But I always liked to get plenty of rest before I staged a Charlie Chaplin hallucination.

Ironically, Sunday morning I thought I was having my own Charlie fantasy. I'd managed to shut off my alarm and go back to sleep, only to have Holly wake me in full tramp costume. She claimed innocence, but I knew she enjoyed giving me gray hair. Just as one should never fry bacon nude, giving apartment keys to grown children is seldom a well thought out plan.

To make amends, Holly fixed lunch while I worked on voiceover commentary for melodious Mark. The goal was far from subtle — have the "spirited" Chuck spout some positives about Mildred and how they maybe even reconnected "upstairs." Then lay it on equally thick about how that swell Professor Caine didn't know diddley about the lost film — other than what Lola herself had shared.

By the time lunch was ready and Holly had changed back into street clothes, I had finished my writing. She was uncharacteristically quiet while we ate, and I assumed she was concerned about getting in harm's way that night.

"You know, we don't have to do this," I said, as I tried to balance a sense of world-weary wisdom with eating a burrito.

"Oh, I'm all right, Dad," she reassured me. "I'm just on my period. I knew I was in trouble last night when I started crying during *The Goonies*. You would have thought it was *Steel Magnolias* meets *Sophie's Choice*, with maybe a *Lifetime* movie thrown in for good measure."

"Well, I don't know, Honey, pirate movies can be emotionally draining."

"Shut up, Pop. Say, what would you think if my Charlie dance involved a variation on his performing waiter routine at the end of *Modern Times*?" As Holly talked she got up from the table and did several

several steps, simultaneously wiggling her nose for potentially amusing mustache movement.

"Charming. We'll have Lola eating right out of our hands."
Holly's mini-performance had us finishing the meal in an upbeat
mood.

Mark arrived shortly after we cleared the table. I did a double take
when I opened the door, while Holly unleashed a high pitched giggle.
He was wearing a hat and coat that could have been hand tailored for
Sherlock Holmes/Basil Rathbone. Indeed, I half expected to hear the
hound of the Baskervilles in the background. Though in Mark's favor,
he had remembered his boom box. But even that only added to the
ludicrousness of his appearance — like Sherlock Holmes had become
a rapper.

"It's too much, isn't it?" he asked, as he came into the living room.

"Just a tad," answered a still chuckling Holly.

Smiling broadly, I suggested, "We might want to brush up on what
it means to go *undercover*."

Taking off his Sherlock duds, he threw himself onto the couch and
momentarily assumed a depressed weak wrist pose. "Just give me a
moment," he said, as he held his hands over his eyes.

Grabbing an imaginary microphone, Holly boomed, "And the
MTV Movie Award winner for the most 'sissyboy sofa scene' goes to
Middletown University's own Mark Roberts."

Mark popped up with the energy level of Jim Carrey's Cuban Pete
in *The Mask* and went into an impromptu acknowledgement shtick, "I
want to thank my mother for dressing me in girl's clothing until I was
twenty-six. I want to thank all my exes for tap dancing on what little
male pride I had left after escaping Momsie. But I want to truly thank
David and Holly for giving my masculinity a second chance as a
semi-tough detective. Because now I can legitimately be called a
dick." With that he bowed and acknowledged the applause of an
imaginary audience.

Holly whistled and yelled "Author, author!" I jumped around
miming a crazed member of the paparazzi. Yes, just another normal
Sunday afternoon in Middletown. Somewhere that crazy couple,
those sociological screwballs Robert and Helen Lynd, were probably
spinning in their graves. But there was no time to check for such minor disturbances in the force. The three musketeers had to rehearse
their Charlie Chaplin revival show. So Holly did her shuffling dance
with the east-west feet, and Mark boomed out his pronouncements
from beyond the grave. As the director, I tried to imagine how this
would best play to an unbalanced woman coming out of a trance-like
state, just after channeling her grandmother.

After three runs through I declared our production ready for opening night. But perfectionist Holly was insecure. "Are you being honest about this, Dad?"

"Who knows? My hunch is yes. But the older I get, the less real life seems. Personally, most of what we're doing is just theory. Remember that George Carlin take on the next life that used to crack me up?"

Holly dutifully recited, "When you die your spirit goes to a garage in upstate New York."

Mark laughed out loud, while I smilingly observed, "That just doesn't seem so far-fetched now, especially after my recent chat with the long-planted Mildred Harris. But I guess this all sounds pretty strange?"

With a wink to Mark, Holly "earnestly" responded, "No, Dad, it actually clears up a lot for me."

Mark quickly added, "For me, too. But you have to promise, no metaphysics about Pee-wee Herman's encounter with Large Marge on the way to the Alamo."

We all laughed, and then discussed whether we should go to the hotel early. My "date" with Lola was still several hours away. But we finally decided it might be helpful to thoroughly case the Skelton suite, not to mention any eavesdropping we could get in on Lola and those new associates.

We went downtown together, but I stayed in the car while they registered and went up to the Lombard suite. Of course, this was one image I didn't need to see — Mark taking my youngest daughter into a hotel. Ironically, they even had my suitcase. Holly had to put her Charlie costume in something. Besides, it was a necessary prop for alleged hotel guests. After about twenty minutes I went up to Holly's Red Skelton suite. Mark was already into his third Midget bottle of booze from the mini-bar, while Holly was camped out on the sofa channel surfing.

The layout for this suite was the same as Lola's — the main door opened into a large fashionable living room area, with a separate bedroom off to the right. But given that the suite was named after patriotic entertainer Skelton, the décor was early American, with a color scheme of earth tone browns. Over the red brick fireplace was a framed, full sheet poster of *A Southern Yankee* — the comedian's greatest film. Holly's big screen television was tucked inside an antique walnut wardrobe, while the mini-bar was built into an old oak ice box.

"Hey, sweet digs, Pop."

"I'm glad you like it. I try to please."

"Yeah, this is one sh-ylist sh-akeout [sic]," slurred a very relaxed Mark.

"Okay, Buddy, maybe we should close ye olde bar. I don't want this to become *Lost Weekend*."

"Dad, before you put Mark in detention, could you score me one of those $6 ginger ales?"

As I got Holly the pricey pop, Mark worked hard to sound normal, "Is that something else to drink?"

"It appears that everything is something you drink. Why don't I just park you in the bedroom for a while?"

While I gently navigated him to the nearest horizontal surface, Mark mumbled to no one in particular, "I'm confused, and I'm going to stay drunk until I'm not confused anymore."

Before joining Holly by the television, I opened the connecting door to the Lombard suite. (Given the more traditional décor of the Skelton layout, this door was not designed to be imperceptible.) I then tiptoed the short interior hall distance to the other connecting door and listened. I could vaguely hear something that sounded like arguing, but it seemed distant, possibly coming from the Lombard bedroom.

I returned to the Skelton suite, got myself a Dr. Pepper (the drink preferred by two-thirds of all academics), and sat down beside Holly. Fittingly, she was watching director Robert Altman's *The Long Goodbye*, an affectionately spoofy updating of Raymond Chandler's novel. Elliott Gould's comically shabby Philip Marlowe pretty much caught the spirit of my little band of three — about to launch a Charlie Chaplin hallucination from a suite named after Red Skelton.

Though totally engrossed in the film, Holly reached over and squeezed my hand a couple of times. She had been fiercely protective of Dad since I had divorced the Wicked Witch of the West two years earlier. I decided to take Holly's lead and watch the picture, too. I hadn't seen it in some time. Plus, I've always liked Gould. I interviewed him years ago, just after he had made it big with *M.A.S.H.*, another Altman film.

The interview was my first freelance piece, two minutes out of college. He could have just given me the brush. I would have. But instead, Gould arranged for us to do the session over lunch, sensing that would be easier for me, which it was. Ironically, ever since Harris' murder I had been thinking about something Gould had said during that meal — "Do people change, or is it that we never really knew what they were like in the first place?" Before Evert's death I thought I knew him so well you could have taken it to the bank. Now, even as Holly and I inched towards this unknown Chaplin film, what I thought I knew could have been so much Sanskrit.

"What's the matter, Dad? Dad?"

"Huh?" I finally managed to grunt.

"You had a funny look on your face, like someone was holding a turd under your nose."

"Oh yeah, sorry about that. I was just wondering if we'd ever get a handle on the real Evert Harris."

"Don't go deep dish on me. I'm just hoping we don't end up smoking a turd in purgatory for the rest of whatever."

"I wouldn't worry about it," I laughed. "If there is a next world, I think everyone is forgiven, other than a few Nazis."

At this precise moment Mark reentered the land of the living by goose-stepping into the living room. Exhibiting neither ill effects of his liquid diet, nor any sense of having been gone more than a heart-beat, he immediately jumped into the conversation with his suggestion of how I should greet the sexy Lola tonight: "I like your ass, could I wear it as a hat?"

Holly nearly snorted ginger ale out her nose, while I experienced the best belly laugh I'd had since the Evert murder mystery had begun. But Mark, like some god of vulgar comedy, simply surveyed his work, saw that it was good, and smiled. Then Holly and I both tackled him into the nearby sofa — sort of a slapstick release before the evening's adventure. It was nearly showtime.

I went next door at exactly eight o'clock, telling my co-conspirators that I would unlock the connecting door as soon as I got a chance. Once again Lola surprised me by leaving the suite's main door slightly ajar. I knocked and slowly entered, closing the door behind me. This time that hard-to-find bedroom door was open and I could see all those flickering candles from two nights before. Entering the bedroom, I was shocked to discover that Lola seemed to have started séance city — the sequel — without me.

Once again she had that pasty vampire-on-a-day-pass look to her, complete with heavy breathing and the skull-like countenance. The room seemed even colder this time. I slowly asked, "Are you here, Mildred?"

A smile flickered across Lola's face, but it was grandmother who answered. "Yes, I have returned, earlier than was expected."

"Why is that?"

"I am not in a good place. My only escape are these fleeting visits."

"Were you and Evert ever close?"

"Yes, he was the only one who really understood me. Evert could always make me laugh. He loved to compose and perform little comic mysteries for me. And his mimicking skills were so inventive you could have thought Charlie was his father. Once he did Basil

Rathbone and Nigel Bruce — you know, Sherlock Holmes and Watson — so perfectly I couldn't stop laughing. Such a dear boy. But I'm afraid my daughter was jealous of her half-brother." Lola/Mildred's eyes closed and tears rolled down her cheeks. "My third husband beat him. I sent him away for his own protection."

"Have you been in contact with Evert since his death?"

"It has not yet been allowed. When one dies —" Frustratingly, Mildred stopped in mid-sentence. Lola's face looked like she was in agony, comparable to when a marathon runner reaches that point called "hitting the wall."

We were about ready to return to regular programming. I raced to the connecting door and let in Holly and Mark. Ushering them into Lola's *Twilight Zone* bedroom, they were both initially stunned by the candle-lit setting, the altar to Mildred, and Lola's appearance.

Positioning Mark behind Lola, our portal to the past, I had him start playing the CD of Chaplin-composed music. I then had Holly, who in full tramp costume and make-up could have been Charlie's twin, begin her *Modern Times* routine directly in front of swami.

There was immediate eye movement on Lola's part. I then motioned for Mark to begin his melodious message about the inherent goodness of Chaplin, coupled with "Professor Caine knows nothing about the lost Chaplin film." The project seemed to be working, like a good B-movie on a limited budget. But a sudden pounding at the door changed all that.

Lola's eyes began to blink and a pronounced shiver went through her body. It was time for the Three Stooges to exit, stage right. (I resisted the temptation to make Curly's "Woo-woo-woo" sound as I ran.) We were out of spook central in record time. Comically, Holly stayed in character, skidding around corners just like Charlie. As we closed the connecting door behind us, we could hear the main door to Lola's suite being forced open.

Chapter 14

There's something about working the streets I like. It's the tramp in me, I suppose.
    — Chaplin's punning Calvero in Limelight *(1952).*

With a door nearly being kicked down right there, I felt as if I'd been working the streets myself. Anyway, while our trio had safely exited Lola's suite, we hung by our connecting door to listen. A voice straight out of *The Godfather* said, "What the Fuck."

This was matched by an equally tough guy rejoinder, "The dead broad has been here. Lola's into that séance shit. She'll come out of it soon enough. Get yourself a beer, I'm going to hit the shower. I told you there was no need to tattoo that door." With the coast apparently clear, we made tracks out of there. (Our only miniscule delay was Mark's need to pirate a souvenir towel.) All three of us returned to our normal reality the following morning with a full schedule of classes. Holly and I planned to regroup in the afternoon, with her staying at my apartment until we figured out the Charlie/Evert movie mystery. I expected Lola to contact me again, but she didn't.

I was, moreover, starting to have concerns over ever cracking the case. I was reminded of, and could relate to, pitcher Dizzy Dean's description of someone slow on the basepaths — "He runs too long in one place — he's gotta lot of up 'n down but not much forward." Holly had expressed the same concern more succinctly that morning, "I hope we can Forrest Gump our way through this."

Thinking back to Mildred's script pages, I shared an old axiom with Holly which seemed timely, "To be ignorant of an object's value is to be ignorant of your own peril."

But my sweet smartass of a daughter made her exit with the flip-pant comeback, "Who said that, Cher?" Family ties are wonderful, yet drop-kicking a loved one has its plusses, too.

My two lecture classes and a discussion session went well, even though I continued to be distracted by recent events. A student's comment, however, comically reminded me of the ease with which violence is accepted in our society. The analysis criticism class was discussing the image of the professor in pop culture, after having seen Michael Caine in *Educating Rita.*

So it was only a matter of time before someone mentioned the professor on *Gilligan's Island.* A seemingly docile student, with a girth to match that of the Skipper, matter-of-factly observed, "Gilligan always screws everything up, like the professor's coconut shell phone system. Why don't they just kill him?"

He got a big laugh and I segued it into more discussion on professors and violence. It seemed fitting, what with Evert's murder and the fact that several of the students had just seen a university screening of *Who's Afraid of Virginia Woolf,* with Richard Burton's academic flirting with offing Elizabeth Taylor. Personally, I think it would have improved the picture but I've never been much of a Taylor fan.

After my discussion class I had two hours before I was supposed to meet Holly, so I asked the department secretary if she knew anything about the "catacombs." To my surprise, Linda said, "All the departments have just recently been assigned cage space down there."

"Cage space?" I asked.

Preoccupied with her computer screen, Linda's answer was little more than an aside, "Yeah, you know, cubicles enclosed in metal grating, sort of like those storage areas some apartments have."

"How long ago did all this transpire?"

With an exasperated, "I swear," Linda complained, "You professors never read department memos. It's been a month or two. Other than poor old Professor Harris, none of you paid any attention."

"Evert asked about cage space in the 'catacombs?'" I said, trying to mask my excitement.

Finally taking her eyes off the screen, this woman with much too heavy a work schedule said, "It was the last thing I did for him."

"How so?"

"I gave him the two department keys and showed him how to go down there. The next thing I know I'm reading 'Harris Murdered.'"

"Do you know if he actually took anything there?"

Clearly, the thought had never occurred to her, because she got all wide-eyed at the suggestion. "Do you think there's a tie-in?" asked Linda breathlessly.

Not wanting to blow my amateur sleuthing cover, I pooh-poohed any connection and attempted to defuse the issue by asking how Evert had returned the keys, since Linda said getting him down there was the last time she'd seen Evert.

Winking at me she shared, "I told him to slide them under my desk mat, since I was just then closing up the office." (Ah yes, Linda's famous film department security system.)

Attempting to further cover my tracks but not really straying too far from the truth, I told Linda I was interested in checking on any lost films the department might have. With that request, she gave me two large keys (gold and gray in color) and directed me to an inconspicuous doorway half-way down the hall from the office. I'd always assumed it was a custodian's supply closet. The gray key got me through the door; the gold one was for the cage.

The stairwell on the other side of the door was circular, with enough cobwebs to make Bela Lugosi proud. The only noise was a humming sound from a distant generator. At the bottom of the stairs was yet another door, painted a bright blue — for no apparent reason, unless a blue fire door struck someone as funny.

The film department cage was the third cubicle beyond the blue door. Opening the lock my heart definitely slid into overdrive, not unlike Cary Grant investigating the locked wine cellar in *Notorious*. It was hard for me to imagine that Evert's Charlie movie might be that close at hand. Could this be the real deal?

Indeed, despite the *Time Machine* poster and script, it was even difficult to visualize Charlie as both Christ and a 13th disciple. I felt a bit like artist Gustave Courbet, who when asked to include angels in a painting, said, "I have never seen an angel. Show me an angel and I will paint one."

My image of Charlie was more the devilish sort. While I had never really second guessed my decision to participate in the birthing of Evert's secret, I was still struggling with the significance of this lost picture. Finding it would turn the history of film comedy on its ear. Regardless, I promised myself to go lightly on the macho bravado, like when I got the gun from the midget.

As if testing my decision to be less than heroic, there was a sudden power outage and the "catacombs" went black. I don't deal well with total darkness. I slept with a nightlight until I was thirty. Darkness is also why I don't go camping. Well, it's that, and the fact I can just as easily have something crawl up my ass at home. Anyway, I told myself to relax, that the power was never out for that long, which it wasn't, and that I should just sit tight. So I leaned against the cage and daydreamed about my bestseller chronicling the discovery of Chaplin's lost Jesus film. Walter Mitty would have been proud. Just when I was about to pick up my Pulitzer Prize I heard the sound of footsteps in the distant darkness.

Who the hell was coming from the other end of the hall? And what was that tiny light accompanying them — no bigger than a lit cigarette but burning more evenly. What should I do? Hide? Find something to use as a weapon? But what? I felt my way along the grating of the cage. My foot struck what appeared to be a piece of two-by-four. I reached down and yes, that's what it was. So there I was standing in the dark making like Mickey Mantle at bat — waiting for a small light to get bigger. As it got closer I raised the two-by-four over my head and wondered if I should rethink my plan to be less heroic.

Just when I was ready to cause a substance resembling guacamole to come out of a heavy's ears I heard, "Hey Pop, is that you? What's with the big stick? Are you going to knock my teeth out and punch me in the stomach for mumbling?" And with that Holly shined her key light in my eyes and smiled. With the most modest of lights, she had obviously not been slowed down by the dark.

"Kiddo, I don't mind tellin' you, you came close to buying the farm. I nearly brained you."

"Aren't you supposed to count three first, like in a movie?"

"Be serious, Holly."

"I'm always serious about movies," she said.

"How'd you find me down here? I thought you had class."

"Our prof didn't show. You don't do that, do you? Anyway, Linda said you were down here. And since you had the keys, she let me in another door down the hall — "

"Take a breath Holly, you're like an auctioneer."

Just then there was a sound like distant thunder and she asked, "What was that?"

"That's the generator kicking in, we should have some lights soon." As if on cue, they came on almost immediately.

"Way to call it, Dad. So should we explore this oversized bird cage?"

"Most definitely." With that I opened the film department cubicle and we began to sort through a mountain of movie stuff jammed in a cage about 15 feet by 10 feet. The space was dominated by eleven filing cabinets which formed a horseshoe-shaped ring around the three sides of the cubicle. Each cabinet had five shelves.

A 16mm feature film is on two to three reels, while a comparable 35mm movie would have twice as many reels. Thus, with seven to ten 16mm pictures per shelf, each cabinet represented potentially 50 films. If Holly and I methodically went through all eleven cabinets we might be looking at as many as 500 plus movies. Ironically, I thought

of a sign one of my grad school professors had in his office —
"FEAR NO ART."

Some films were in large metal cans and clearly marked. But the
majority were merely stacked on reels, with the title on the leader of
the film stock. Unfortunately, many department features were un-
marked. This necessitated unwinding several feet of film and checking individual movie frames to figure out what the picture was. Since
all the department films were classics, this was not as hard as it
seemed. Well, not for film geeks like Holly and me.

We were slowly and methodically working through the cabinets
one by one. "How many movies have we checked now, Pop?"

"I think we're at something like 100, give or take a few. Why, are
you getting hungry?"

"No, I knocked off a shake before I came down. Besides, I feel
like a Blues Brother — 'on a mission from God.'"

"Nicely put."

"Do you miss showing films, as opposed to using DVDs for
classes?"

"If the print quality is superior, by all means. But sadly, most university film departments were usually strapped for money, and had to
depend upon a limited movie library of mediocre prints. I remember
in grad school we had a copy of *Birth of a Nation* which was so old it
might have been D. W. Griffith's personal copy."

Laughing, Holly said, "Okay, I get the picture." We worked silently for maybe ten minutes more when she suddenly shouted,
though we were no more than five feet apart, "Hey, get a load of
this!"

With two hands she gave me a titleless film can which initially
looked no different than the others. . .until I saw the same logo which
had been embossed on the leather case holding Mildred's script —
Charlie's cane, derby, and boots.

Holly started to jump up and down with joy, like a five-year-old at
her birthday party, "So open it, Pop!"

"Alright already, keep your socks on," I said, smiling. Hurrying, I
cut my finger on the sharp edges of the can's lid. "Damn." Prying it
open, there were two 16mm reels of film — approximately 90 minutes.

Since commercial movies are shot on 35mm, Chaplin, or someone
(possibly Evert?) had transferred it to 16mm. However, maybe Chaplin never planned to release it, shooting the film as merely an elaborate home movie. During the 1920s, when the picture would have
been made, 16mm was the home movie format. And historically,
Chaplin was later famous for appearing in the home movies of others,
such as the comic bits he improvised for the amateur camera of actor

Ken Murray, who is best known now as a popular television entertainer of the 1950s.

Unspooling some of the film, Holly and I bumped heads in our joint haste to take a look at what might be Chaplin's Jesus movie.

"Fucking A Dad!"

"Holly!"

"Sorry," she mumbled, "I didn't realize I was auditory."

"Yeah, right," I said. "Now I'm going to sneak a peek, and after I faint, you can take a look, too." With that, I carefully unrolled about three feet of film and held it up to the overhead light. While there was no *Charlie Chaplin and the Time Machine* opening title on the film stock, there was a brief prologue which said:

> The Tramp visits the home of his good friend H. G. Wells and is warned by the author/inventor to 'never go near his laboratory time machine.'"

This was followed by footage of an odd looking little vehicle that resembled an exercise bike encased in a glass bubble.

I excitedly turned to Holly and said, "Break out the champagne, this is definitely it!"

"Let me see! Let me see!" was all she could say. So I carefully gave her the reel, while I picked up the second one in the film can. And bingo, I had a second pleasant surprise — there was a short note from Evert attached to the bottom of the can.

> David — Congrats! I hope you found this challenge from a dead man entertaining. When you write your book about all this, and I know you will, please note that while my mother, Mildred Harris (the co-star of this Chaplin film), and I had issues, I still loved her very much.
>
> Life, unlike an old-fashioned detective story, means we often have to live without all the answers. But once you watch this picture you'll understand why it was a bit too personal for me to bring to the world. You, on the other hand, will be the perfect person for the job. So do me proud, and have a great life. Who knows, if there is a God (and He likes movies), maybe we'll meet up again. . .with Chaplin in tow!
>
> —Evert (somewhere in the The Elysian Fields)

I digested this in a visual gulp but when I started to share the note with Holly the lights went off yet again. I had a bad feeling about it. And my bad feeling was more than just that old fear-of-the-dark thing.

Chapter 15

[H. G.] Wells tries on my hat, then takes my cane and twirls it. The effect is ridiculous, especially as just at the moment I notice the two volumes of the Outline of History *on his table.*
  —*Chaplin on his 1921 visit with Wells.*

"Here we go again," was Holly's only comment when the lights went off. But I was more concerned than that, as the little hairs stood up on the back of my neck. Moreover, my ears perked up for any new threatening sounds.

Without saying as much, I asked Holly, "Do you still have that little key light handy?"

"Yeah, what's up? Do you want to split? Hey, I've got my sweat pants on — we could get something to eat."

With Evert's Charlie film in hand, we slowly and carefully made our way out of the cage area guided by that tiny beam of light. Even then, I managed to trip as we left the cubicle. "Did I tell you, I'm also a clown with the circus?"

"Gee, Dad, I just thought you were a bad dancer."

Before I could respond there was the sound of a metal door opening at the end of the hall and the unmistakable voice of Lola ordering someone to "Find them; I want to know if they've got the film!"

"Whatever they're selling," I whispered to Holly, "I'm not interested." As we turned and hurried for the door closest to us we no longer needed her key light. Lola, with a scared Linda from the office in tow, and whoever else had joined our Evert/Charlie scavenger hunt, was shining an industrial strength beam of light our way. Once more I felt like Holly and I were living on the blade of a knife — the proverbial easy target.

Once through the blue door, we momentarily returned to near blackness. But there was enough light coming through a window in the ground floor door, at the top of the stairs, to guide us back to the main hall.

Not wanting an instant replay of the Munchkin shooting, Holly and I sprinted for the main exit. Our only plan, or hope, was to get away. Outside the door we had a lifesaving surprise — James Schickel's limo was at the curb and he was halfway up the walk coming our way.

Holly and I proceeded to sprint towards him, causing him to pause with an incredulous look on his face. "Do you give all campus visitors such a wonderful welcome?" he asked.

Gasping for breath, I half shouted, "We've got the Chaplin film but Lola Hopper and some goons are right behind us!"

With a clipped, "Say no more," he motioned us to make for the car while he surprised me by pulling out a *Dirty Harry* sized gun and covering our retreat. Piling into the back of the limo we quickly turned to see what Schickel would do.

Full of surprises, he actually shot the first person through the door in the leg. The hood, who appeared to be holding a gun, hit the sidewalk just as his partner came out. He skidded to a halt like a cartoon character and dove back into the building. When nobody else came out (gunfire often has that effect), Schickel slowly backed his way to the limo and climbed in the passenger section with us. No sooner had the door closed than Jeeves took off like a blue streak.

Instead of going to Schickel's museum-like country home, we went to what he called a "safe house" in the city. Nondescript from the outside, it was predictably movie-related on the inside, with framed original posters and other cinema art work covering almost every square inch of wall space. The place no doubt belonged to a film colleague, or maybe it was just Schickel's townhouse. We never found out. . .never really asked, I guess. As they say, life begins when you start minding your own business.

Very little had been said in the car. But as soon as we entered the house he asked, "Are you sure this is it?"

Nodding yes while still gripping the film can I asked, "How did you just happen to be in front of the building when we came tearing out?"

Smiling he said, "I might be an old reclusive film buff but I still have a few teeth in my head and friends around town. I hear things."

Smiling back at him I asked, "What'd ya hear?"

"The word was Hopper had some new strongmen, and was anxious to put an end to operation Charlie."

"That's a bit thin but I'll let it pass," I said, aping Bogart. "So how does that bring you to my department building?"

With a self-conscious exhaling of breath he patiently observed, "David, you're not going to make me say I'm sorry for saving you two."

"Lighten up, Pop," said Holly. "Without Mr. Schickel we'd probably be road kill right now."

Responding to Holly but speaking to Schickel I said, "Sorry, it's just that big ass guns . . . ."

"Guns don't kill people. . .postal workers do, oh, and people in Little Debbie trucks," interrupted Holly with a smirk.

Laughing, I replied, "Oh, that'll bring the sun out, Sweetie."

Joining in, Schickel said, "As the old saying goes, 'You can't make an omelet without jeopardizing the lives of a few innocent people.'"

"It's not my fault," I alibied, "my mother was off her nut — always thought she'd left the iron on."

"Okay, enough with this *Evening at the Improv* shtick. Do you think we were followed?" Holly asked.

"My driver is good at losing people," said Schickel.

"Do you have any special security here?" I asked.

"What is this, the original *Scarface*? Would you two relax," Schickel answered.

"Okay, I guess I can breathe a little easier," said Holly. "How about we watch the Charlie movie?"

"Yes, by all means," said Schickel.

"Where to?" I asked.

"Follow me," was his answer. And Schickel proceeded to take us to a screening room on the second floor. Once there he asked, "David?"

"Yes," I said.

"I could really use the movie now. You know, to thread it up and all." I was still clutching the film can as tightly as when Holly and I dashed out of the film department building.

Embarrassed, I said, "Yes, of course." But even then it was difficult to let go. Gee, I was almost as bad as the dead midget. I remember having to pry Mildred's script out of his tight little hands. Maybe I should look into a new lifestyle that doesn't require my presence.

As Schickel went to the small projection booth in the back of the room, Holly and I waited with wide-eyed excitement. A million questions bounced around in my head. Would the movie be as provocatively entertaining as we hoped, or had its non-release been predicated on Chaplin disappointment with the finished product?

What about Lola's take on her grandmother Mildred? Would *Charlie and the Time Machine* have made Harris a star and/or established her as a major silent screen actress?

What of Chaplin's two roles? Would his Charlie, the 13th disciple, match the magic of his Tramp parts? Of course, maybe I've put the man on too high a pedestal. As Mrs. Einstein once said to her husband, "What the hell do you know?"

Having read Mildred's script material had increased my interest, if that was possible. But it didn't really tell me how effective an affectionately satirical Jesus story would be. The beauty of Chaplin's gloves-off Nazi satire in *The Great Dictator* was that everyone loves to hate Hitler.

My thoughts were interrupted at this point by Schickel's raised voice from the all-glass projection booth, "All set?" After Holly and I nodded in unison, the lights dimmed and we were ready to start. Following the aforementioned prologue (briefly examined in the "catacombs"), where Charlie is warned to stay away from H. G. Wells' time machine, the story which unfolds has the Tramp as a houseguest of the famous sci fi/fantasy author.

It appeared that Chaplin had managed to get the real H. G. Wells to appear at the start of the picture. The shooting of such a scene possibly occurred during the comedian's 1921 visit to London when he first met with the author. Regardless, the opening presented Wells giving Charlie a tour of his mansion.

The high point of their stroll was the stop at the writer's lab, where he showed Charlie his time machine. On the big screen it didn't so much resemble an exercise bike in a bubble as a miniature helicopter without a rotor blade.

Though the picture began with a prologue warning for Charlie to stay clear of the time machine, during Wells' nickel tour he humored the Tramp by allowing him to sit in the device. And then a series of titles briefly explained how the time machine worked. There were two keys. One was the *vaporizer equalizer*, which triggered the rapid revolutions of the capsule — enabling it to slingshot itself through time. If turned left, the traveler went back in time. The opposite direction sent him back to the future.

The other key was the *time gauge*, which allowed a traveler to set the target year. Speed of travel was 60 years per minute. A third gauge, without a key, was the *location setting device*. It need only be activated if one wanted to also visit a different part of the globe during the time travel.

After this time tripping tutorial, Wells and Charlie have a midnight snack and then the author walks the little fellow to a guest bedroom. But the Tramp can't sleep, so he gets a book from a nearby table, which turns out to be Wells' real-life 1921 bestseller *The Outline of History*. Charlie randomly turns to a section on "The Scriptures and the Prophets." And as he begins to read about Jesus, he falls into a deep sleep.

"In slumberland," as Chaplin's film title describes it, Charlie's fascination with the time machine mixes with the Jesus readings to produce a dream where the little fellow becomes a time traveler. Sneaking into Wells' lab, he gets into the machine and sets the *time gauge* key for 30 AD, which a title tells us "was when Jesus began his teachings." He then programs the *location setting device* for the Holy Land. Next, Charlie turns the *vaporizer equalizer* to the left.

The bubbled machine begins to spin like a top, and the capsule-like portion of the screen goes to red. Chaplin had apparently had this section hand-tinted, a technique sometimes used by pioneering film-makers. Because a hand-coloring process can never be uniform from film frame to film frame, it produces a pulsating effect which can be quite charming. Indeed, for a time tripping character, it could not have been more appropriate.

As a backdrop to the spinning time machine, various images from Middle Eastern history flash by, starting with apparition-like illuminations of a World War I era Lawrence of Arabia. Ultimately, the machine's revolutions start to slow down. But the location has now changed from H. G. Wells' lab to a desert setting in Biblical times.

As Charlie pops out of the capsule he continues to spin, ultimately falling on his keister. As he struggles to his feet to get the *time gauge* key from the machine he inadvertently touches the capsule. The Tramp immediately pulls his hand back and starts to blow on his fingers — the time machine is obviously hot.

The movie then cuts to Christ addressing a large multitude, only it's Chaplin as Jesus. But just as that fact starts to sink in, the camera slowly pans to the back of the gathering — revealing the Tramp as the 13th disciple in a robe and sandals trying to get a better view. But he spends most of his time shuffling around the outskirts of the throng, never quite satisfied with his place in the crowd.

The film dissolves to the following day, with Jesus/Chaplin speaking from a fishing boat to a sizeable gathering on the shore. Charlie is first referred to in a screen title as the "13th disciple." He seems to be responsible for keeping the boat relatively stationary, despite the fact it's anchored. This involves Charlie's use of a large paddle, which ultimately sends him into the water. Once again Chaplin seems to play it safe by keying more upon Charlie the antiheroic disciple instead of his relatively straight rendition of Christ.

There were several such scenes along these lines in the next thirty odd minutes of film, with the most amusing take being Charlie's response to Christ/Chaplin turning the water into wine at the wedding party. The little fellow is simply incredulous about what has transpired — scratching his head and attempting to replicate the miracle himself when no one is watching. (I was reminded of the later "Sorcerer's Apprentice" portion of *Fantasia,* when Mickey Mouse attempts to duplicate the magic of the master.) Ultimately, the segment ends with Jesus leading the weavingly hammered Charlie home in the desert night.

Shortly after this, Chaplin's Jesus meets Mildred Harris' Mary Magdalene at the well. This is soon followed by the comic rescue of Mary from the stone-throwers. In both scenes, Mildred's Mary is a very fragile birdlike presence, emulating the popular 1920s acting style of Lillian Gish. In contrast, Chaplin's Christ is extremely physical and impassioned — lecturing the crowd with the same fervor as the Tramp's pep talk to Paulette Goddard's sexy gamin at the close of *Modern Times.*

As the crucifixion approaches, the scenes fluctuate between broad comedy (Charlie disastrously assisting Jesus the carpenter) and somber recreations of famous artistic renderings of Christ — such as a variation upon Leonardo da Vinci's *Last Supper.* In the serious scenes, Chaplin apes the silent film style of D. W. Griffith in *Birth of a Nation* — movie title cards include footnote-like documentation on the exactitude of each historical recreation.

The actual crucifixion is shot in close-up, with cutaways to both Mary and disciple Charlie at the base of the cross. Chaplin seems to have declared a moratorium on his signature style of energized characters in this scene. Consequently, all three figures appear to be in a subdued state of grace. Moreover, consistent with Chaplin's own tendencies, his performance as Christ on the cross turns the savior into an immense emotional being, rather than a religious icon. There is such a natural intensity in his ability to feel and suffer that his close-ups of Christ almost glow — not unlike the tramp's later torment at the conclusion of *City Lights,* after losing the once blind girl. This emotional close-up intensity anticipates Carl Dreyer's silent master piece, *The Passion of Joan of Arc,* where actress Maria Falconetti literally radiates in her Jesus-like martyrdom. Could Dreyer have somehow seen Chaplin's film on Christ?

Chaplin as Christ is eventually approached on the cross by an apparent guardian angel in the guise of a beautiful young girl. The part is played by Lita Grey, who had just been the flirting angel in *The Kid,* and in real life would soon become the second Mrs. Chaplin. The comedian's Christ accepts her offer to rescue Him and showcases immense relief that He no longer must die for humanity's sins. Jesus then imagines what a normal life might be like for a mere mortal.

What follows are some of Mildred's most entertaining scenes as a somewhat loopy wife, assisting and/or frustrating Jesus both around the house and in the carpenter shop. She seems to be playing a variation upon Charlie's antiheroic "13th disciple."

By the time of the potentially blasphemous love making scene, it has been firmly established that Christ and Mary are in a loving relationship. Surprisingly, the sex scene, while tastefully shot, is neither short, nor photographed in shadow. Running several minutes in length, this portrayal of a lovemaking Christ briefly reveals both performers in full frontal nudity. The term *riveting* does not come close to describing the scene. First, it's Jesus in the sex act. Second, it's cinema's most celebrated star in a nude love scene. (And the movie fleetingly documents that this famous Hollywood Romeo was as well-endowed as the gossip sheets suggested.) Third, while often erotic, there is also a great deal of comedy, such as an excited Christ/Chaplin occasionally popping out of their bedding to flex his undersized arm muscles — an antiheroic macho man. And fourth, Mildred as Mary is stunning, both in her lovely lithe form, and the poignant attention she gives Christ/Chaplin. One senses she wasn't acting but rather revealing her love for Chaplin. Though the picture clearly belongs to Chaplin in his dual roles, in this provocative scene Mildred holds her own with cinema's greatest figure. It is daring footage for even a filmmaker of today. In the early 1920s, the scene would have caused riots.

After this provocative portion of the film, there is a lengthy montage of Jesus, Mary, and the disciple Charlie growing older. On Christ's apparent deathbed an angry but still youthful Judas appears, played with swashbuckling verve by Chaplin's real-life best friend, Douglas Fairbanks, Sr.

He shouts, "Traitor!" at Chaplin's Christ, and through titles it is revealed that the earlier guardian angel was actually Satan in disguise. Chaplin's Jesus movingly accepts his holy responsibilities and suddenly He is transformed back to the cross. The picture then cuts to a long take of Charlie comically scrambling through the desert. Ultimately, he stops near a large rock formation and after removing some brush, a cave is revealed.

Charlie pulls the time machine out and climbs into the single seat enclosed by the bubble. He inserts the *time gauge* key and sets the date for 1921 (Holly and I had been right!), and the *location setting device* for London. The little fellow then turns the *vaporizer equalizer* to the right (for the future). As the time machine begins to shake, prior to those rapid revolutions, the picture dissolves back to Charlie in bed being shaken awake by H. G. Wells. The accompanying title has the author telling the little fellow, "You were having a bad dream,

Old Man."

The movie then cuts to a very startled expression on Charlie's face. Followed by a double-take glance at Wells' *Outline of History*, which is still on his bed. As "The End" flashes across the screen and Schickel brings up both the house lights and the retractable screen it's our turn to do a double-take — an armed Lola, flanked by her two goons, were standing just where the screen had been.

Chapter 16

"I've never liked surprises."
    Chaplin in a 1917 letter to Mildred
    Harris, prior to their marriage.

I've never been so dumbfounded. And from the shocked look on Holly's face I'm sure she felt the same. When I turned towards the back of the room even Schickel looked like he'd had a bad piece of fish.

"Okay everybody, front and center," said an angry sounding Lola. "And Schickel, keep your hands above your head." The thugs on either side of her were straight out of B-movie central casting, complete with tough guy scowls and drawn guns. Very film noirishe.

As we came forward to thug-land, walking along one side of the theatre, Lola went back to the projection booth along the opposite wall. She was after the Chaplin film. In no time at all she rejoined us downfront, with the movie clutched to her chest.

Lola's anger was contagious. I suddenly felt pissed that she was in our faces again. I found myself saying to her, "Shouldn't you be out burning crosses, or training pit bulls?"

Schickel, quickly tried to play diplomat by asking the question on all our minds — "What are you going to do with that film?"

A still seemingly livid Lola, what my mom would have described as "spitting nails," growled, "I'm going to destroy it!"

"No!" Holly, Schickel, and I fairly shouted in unison.

Then, "Why would you do that?" Holly cried.

Ignoring a straight answer, she said, "This should be the happiest day of my life. I've finally been able to track down and see this damn picture. This should have been my grandmother's day, too — vindicated after all these years."

"It still could be," pleaded Holly.

"Shut up! Chaplin screwed us one more time, the stanky little shit! The footage my mother said grandmother talked about wasn't there. Even in death the bastard denied us —"

"But," I interrupted, "Mildred is charming in the love scene and several of those slapstick interludes."

"Interludes! They're fucking interludes! Her legacy was supposed to be a much longer sex scene which focuses on Mildred, and provided artistic cutaways of her as a transition device throughout the movie, like D. W. Griffith did with the rocking cradle in *Intolerance*. I can't build a case for a neglected silent career from this!"

"But surely you wouldn't flush what little legacy she has. This Jesus film will be huge!" Holly pleaded.

"Didn't I already tell you to shut up!" snapped Lola.

"Idiot," said Holly softly.

"What?" asked Lola.

"Idiot *Savant*, I was thinking how Savant-like you are, in the best sense of the word," Holly alibied, with the moxie of a blind burglar.

Lola quickly came right up to Holly and slapped her soundly. I grabbed Holly and held her, since I had sadly never schooled her in the dangers of sassing your basic killer type.

Schickel, again trying to play peacemaker, said, "It's obviously a valuable movie. Isn't there some sort of possible trade-off? Couldn't we somehow make it up to you?"

"You're making it up pretty good so far," Lola said.

At that comment, Lola and Schickel just stared at each other. The silence grew, as did my confusion over the scene playing out here. Finally, I said, "So, Lola, let's drop the cat and mouse game. Doesn't this mean you killed Harris, or had him killed, for nothing?"

"It wasn't me honey," she said. "That jerk Evert was alive and mocking me the last time we met." And then turning her attention back to Schickel, she said, "And you, Schickel, have been an even worse pain in the ass — rescuing these two boobs with the clues out of my reach every time they got close to putting their hands on grandmother's movie."

She had given Holly and me such a look when she said, 'these two boobs' — that my understanding of the picture was slowly coming into focus. Was it possible that Hopper and Schickel had *both* been following us from friggin' clue to friggin' clue all over campus and the state of Indiana? Whereas Lola's desperate, armed killer Buick approach was thoroughly scary and kept Holly and me perversely determined to succeed, Schickel's frequent 11th hour rescues now seemed even more sinister and I hadn't suspected a thing. But the penny finally dropped and I knew that I truly had been a dumb boob, until now. I'll just call Holly an innocent chip off the old boob.

If Schickel and Lola were both bad guys from different camps, I had to ask, "So you killed Evert, didn't you, Schickel?"

He couldn't meet my eyes. Instead, he slowly shuffled his feet and studied the floor. Holly jumped out of my embrace and the Mafia twins nearly had dueling coronaries snapping to attention. But for once she was too shocked to speak. Silence isn't always golden. It can be oppressively anxious. Even Lola was waiting for his answer.

Speaking so quietly one had to strain to hear him, Schickel finally muttered, "I had done so much for him and his fucking endowed chair. Even the purchase of that damned Maltese Falcon I had arranged for him at a fraction of its true value. But he wouldn't give an inch on the Christ film. . .just wanted me to be a glorified clue master, and I lost control. But I never planned to kill him. You take stuff just so long, and then something snaps. I got so angry that night and it happened. . .killed him with that Falcon."

"Don't get all weepy on us, Old Man. You did me a favor. He was never much of an uncle. And he always played dumb ass about the Chaplin film with me, too."

With my mouth hanging so far open I found it hard to form words, I finally managed to stammer, "Would, would you have killed us, too?"

Without looking at me, but with the first sense of emotion in his voice, Schickel shared, "I really hoped it would never come to that."

"Oh, that's comforting!" said an angry Holly.

Still not believing Schickel's involvement, I half asked, "But you seemed to be in on Harris' plan, including the Chaplin script pages."

"I was only a player. . .maybe a bit more informed, but a player just the same," he answered. Evert and I had been friendly rivals a long time. We couldn't foresee how I would end that relationship." He paused again before he continued. "And as his final spit-in-the-face gesture, Evert gave the clues to you, David, instead of me. My offered help along the way was genuine, because I knew that together we would find it."

Holly interjected, "But you had so much, that museum-like house, all those priceless posters, lobby cards . . ."

"Sadly," said Schickel, "collectors never have enough. That's the nature of collecting. A sorry business, actually."

"And you would have killed us over the Chaplin film?" Holly's manner had changed from anger to sadness.

"You know," said a suddenly philosophical Schickel, "I don't much like modern movies. But there's one, *Chinatown*, which suits this situation. Late in that film John Huston observes, 'Most people never have to face the fact that at the right time and the right place they are capable of anything.'"

"What about the midget?" I asked. "Did you kill him, too?"

Without saying word one he simply looked in Lola's direction. As if taking this as a cue she said, "That would be my doing. He was a weasel; a weasel with no balls. He'd bungled it and I couldn't tolerate it. He got what he deserved. But don't worry, none of you are on my hit list, unless you try to stop me from leaving with this film." And with that she and the Mafia twins started out of the room.

As they rushed past our little trio of unarmed, hands-in-the-air types, Schickel borrowed a move from Laurel & Hardy and tripped Lola (who was then literally airborne — we're talking *Where Eagles Dare* territory). He then caught the flying canister and screamed, "You can't destroy it!"

About the time Lola returned from orbit (again, we're talking what seemed like days here — Stan & Ollie would have been proud. . .jealous even), the nearest of her goodfellas shot Schickel twice at point-blank range to the gut. The two gunmen laughed as Schickel slowly sank to the floor with the film, and just laid there. Holly and I were too shocked to move. In fact, Holly later counted it as a moral victory she hadn't soiled herself.

Lola, however, had recovered from her surprise launching, and cussing like a sailor, she was soon bent over Schickel to retrieve the film. Instead, she let out a scream as he grabbed her by the hair and roughly pulled her down to him. He had her throat in a choking bear hug and yelled, "Drop your guns, boys, or the lady stops breathing."

Schickel had Holly and me pick up the weapons, as well as hang on to the film can. As he released a very pissed Lola to join her side-kicks, under my gun-in-hand guard duty, Schickel said, "I've got to sit down."

I couldn't help noticing that the film canister had a large new dent on the edge. But as I started to compliment Schickel on his luck I only then saw how much blood had soaked through his shirt.

"Holly," I said, "Call 911 — tell them we need an ambulance and the cops. The phone's by the door we came in."

As Holly dashed to call, I directed my attention to Schickel, "We've got to get some pressure on that."

Turning to Lola's "goodfellas," I couldn't resist telling the one who'd snickered first when Schickel was shot, "Yo, Guido, toss him your coat. And be quick about it."

"You gotta be kidding. He's just sitting there to save funeral ex-penses."

"How should I say this," I replied, "unless you want to sleep with the fishes, fuckface, you'll toss your jacket to Mr. Schickel NOW!"

Like magic, the coat was soon in the air, with the old man then using it to apply pressure to the wound.

Wow, me bossing gangsters. If nobody knew fear they wouldn't know how nice it is to feel in charge. I wondered if I should start having people kiss my ring? Or maybe, in Raymond Chandler fashion, I'd just start referring to any tough guy as "soldier."

Holly ran in just after this, and started helping with Schickel. "The ambulance is on the way," she gasped, "and the cops, too."

While we sat tight waiting for the authorities I caught Guido's sidekick, let's call him Sonny, silently mouthing the words "Fuck me" to Holly.

Shockingly, I saw her approach him and plant a hand on each of his shoulders. Startled speechless, before I could say anything she brought her right knee up hard and fast between his legs. As Sonny let out a pained gasp and collapsed to the floor holding his privates, Holly said, "There, now you're fucked."

Unfortunately, this unexpected entertainment distracted me from Lola. The woman had gone from advanced pissed, to sobbing. Whether those tears had been a cover, we'll probably never know. But I caught her going for something inside her coat.

"Stop!" I shouted, but when Lola continued, I shot her in the right shoulder. The hand inside her coat fell to Lola's side, apparently empty. "Oh my God," I mumbled, "I've shot an unarmed asshole."

"Look again, Pop," said Holly.

Peering closer, I was relieved to see a small derringer in Lola's hand. But my comfort zone was quickly dissipated by her angry voice, "You academic fuck, you're dead." And with that, she slowly started to raise the derringer.

"Put it down!" I shouted.

Almost simultaneously, Holly was screaming, "Daddy, shoot, shoot!"

I didn't fire until Lola's arm was almost fully extended. Then I had no other choice. But the shooting came much easier than I would have thought — all the anger and frustration came pouring out. And I just kept firing the gun until the remaining five chambers were empty.

I was no marksman, but at point-blank range it wasn't all that hard. The difficult part came later, trying to live down the memory of her macabre dance of death. It was not unlike the deadly gyrations which chronicle the end of *Bonnie and Clyde* in Arthur Penn's darkly comic biography film of the duo.

Moments after I'd reduced Lola to so much Swiss cheese (smoke was still swirling from my gun barrel), two cops came bursting into the room with extended arms holding guns big enough to bring down a Mack truck.

"Put the weapon down!" they yelled almost in unison. But I was only too happy to comply. One of the officers turned out to be the university cop (Roberts) who had interviewed me after the break in at my office.

"Are you okay, Professor?" he asked.

"Yeah," I answered, "but she isn't."

Epilogue

In time I again appreciated a happy line from Britain's World War I era song about the Tramp: "Oh the moon shines bright on Charlie Chaplin. . . ."

It has now been a year since the shooting. The initial notoriety of the incident, and the revelations about Chaplin's Jesus film, put Holly and me in the news big time. Plus, we made the talk show circuit, including *Letterman* and *Oprah*. I even turned down a chance to do *Saturday Night Live*. Don't get me wrong, I love the show. But they wanted me to play Sam Peckinpah, Jr., after the director famous for his artful bloodbaths á la *The Wild Bunch* and *Straw Dogs*. The *SNL* sketch would have had me also be a bloody action director. But it seemed a little too grisly to play upon my shooting of Lola.

I did, however, sign a sweet two book contract with a major publishing house. One text will chronicle the mystery search for the Jesus film. The second volume will be a close analysis of the movie and its ties to other Chaplin pictures.

The film itself, *Charlie and the Time Machine*, has its first public screening next month at New York's Lincoln Center. (It took longer because the movie needed major restoration.) Part of the money raised by the Lincoln Center showing will go towards an endowed chair in memory of Evert Harris. His murderer, James Schickel, survived the shooting and is now serving a life sentence at Joliet (Illinois), where he also doubles as the projectionist on movie night. I still can't believe he turned out to be a bad guy. Holly and I really liked him.

My investigative partner/daughter is temporarily putting her college career on hold to write a children's mystery book. Not surprisingly, the central characters are a crime solving father-daughter duo. If successful, the publisher promises it might become a series — so move over Sherlock Holmes. (Something tells me I'll probably end up as the Watson character.)

I don't know if I've rehashed everything exactly as it happened. But it's how I remember it, memory being what passes for personalized reality in life. Like director Kurosawa's *Rashomon*, which explores four characters' varying takes on the same incident, Holly's spin on the preceding events would no doubt have its differences. You'll have to ask her yourself. But as an artist once observed (I think it was Picasso or maybe it was my barber), "Art is a lie that tells the truth." Or, screw the details. While looking back is not without its dangers (remember what happened to Lot's wife), it's something that defines me.

After I finish writing these two contracted for books, I think the next project will be turning this Chaplin murder mystery stuff into a novel. I've written a lot of columns, papers, books, and even letters to the utility companies. But stealing a novel from reality would be. . .well, novel for me. And we'll trust that our hero (moi) lives happily ever after (ain't fiction grand?).

Still, I'm not unlike the central character in Walter Percy's novel *The Moviegoer* — who and what I am is forever connected with film. My favorite pieces of time are not just memories; they are *movie memories* — from my thoughts of a dear grandfather forever being linked to his love of Laurel & Hardy, to Holly's current movie take on our adventure. That is, when discussing this quest for the lost Chaplin film, she entertainingly recycles Bogart's closing line from her favorite film, *The Maltese Falcon*. Describing the allure of that picture's black statuette, Bogie observes, "The stuff that dreams are made of." Thus, you could say that his summation also applies to finding the Chaplin film. In fact, I just did.

Well, this is where the film fades to black, and the theme music crescendos to a satisfying finale, if you're into that sort of thing. But I'll have to give you a rain check on closing comic outtakes, since I'm still tabulating my *life mistakes* — which, if I were a movie director, would definitely be my oeuvre.

Just remember, as a corollary to poet Robert Frost's "The Road Not Taken," sometimes the difference in life isn't so much in selecting the less traveled path but rather how you respond to fellow travelers on any path. Until then, I'll see you at the movies.

THE END

RAMBLE HOUSE's

HARRY STEPHEN KEELER WEBWORK MYSTERIES

(RH) indicates the title is available ONLY in the RAMBLE HOUSE edition

The Ace of Spades Murder
The Affair of the Bottled Deuce (RH)
The Amazing Web
The Barking Clock
Behind That Mask
The Book with the Orange Leaves
The Bottle with the Green Wax Seal
The Box from Japan
The Case of the Canny Killer
The Case of the Crazy Corpse (RH)
The Case of the Flying Hands (RH)
The Case of the Ivory Arrow
The Case of the Jeweled Ragpicker
The Case of the Lavender Gripsack
The Case of the Mysterious Moll
The Case of the 16 Beans
The Case of the Transparent Nude (RH)
The Case of the Transposed Legs
The Case of the Two-Headed Idiot (RH)
The Case of the Two Strange Ladies
The Circus Stealers (RH)
Cleopatra's Tears
A Copy of Beowulf (RH)
The Crimson Cube (RH)
The Face of the Man From Saturn
Find the Clock
The Five Silver Buddhas
The 4th King
The Gallows Waits, My Lord! (RH)
The Green Jade Hand
Finger! Finger!
Hangman's Nights (RH)
I, Chameleon (RH)
I Killed Lincoln at 10:13! (RH)
The Iron Ring
The Man Who Changed His Skin (RH)
The Man with the Crimson Box
The Man with the Magic Eardrums
The Man with the Wooden Spectacles
The Marceau Case
The Matilda Hunter Murder

The Monocled Monster
The Murder of London Lew
The Murdered Mathematician
The Mysterious Card (RH)
The Mysterious Ivory Ball of Wong Shing Li (RH)
The Mystery of the Fiddling Cracksman
The Peacock Fan
The Photo of Lady X (RH)
The Portrait of Jirjohn Cobb
Report on Vanessa Hewstone (RH)
Riddle of the Travelling Skull
Riddle of the Wooden Parrakeet (RH)
The Scarlet Mummy (RH)
The Search for X-Y-Z
The Sharkskin Book
Sing Sing Nights
The Six From Nowhere (RH)
The Skull of the Waltzing Clown
The Spectacles of Mr. Cagliostro
Stand By—London Calling!
The Steeltown Strangler
The Stolen Gravestone (RH)
Strange Journey (RH)
The Strange Will
The Straw Hat Murders (RH)
The Street of 1000 Eyes (RH)
Thieves' Nights
Three Novellos (RH)
The Tiger Snake
The Trap (RH)
Vagabond Nights (Defrauded Yeggman)
Vagabond Nights 2 (10 Hours)
The Vanishing Gold Truck
The Voice of the Seven Sparrows
The Washington Square Enigma
When Thief Meets Thief
The White Circle (RH)
The Wonderful Scheme of Mr. Christopher Thorne
X. Jones—of Scotland Yard
Y. Cheung, Business Detective

Keeler Related Works

A To Izzard: A Harry Stephen Keeler Companion by Fender Tucker — Articles and stories about Harry, by Harry, and in his style. Included is a compleat bibliography.

Wild About Harry: Reviews of Keeler Novels — Edited by Richard Polt & Fender Tucker — 22 reviews of works by Harry Stephen Keeler from *Keeler News*. A perfect introduction to the author.

The Keeler Keyhole Collection: Annotated newsletter rants from Harry Stephen Keeler, edited by Francis M. Nevins. Over 400 pages of incredibly personal Keeleriana.

Fakealoo — Pastiches of the style of Harry Stephen Keeler by selected demented members of the HSK Society. Updated every year with the new winner.

Strands of the Web: Short Stories of Harry Stephen Keeler — 29 stories, just about all that Keeler wrote, are edited and introduced by Fred Cleaver.

RAMBLE HOUSE's LOON SANCTUARY

A Clear Path to Cross — Sharon Knowles short mystery stories by Ed Lynskey.

A Jimmy Starr Omnibus — Three 40s novels by Jimmy Starr.

A Niche in Time and Other Stories — Classic SF by William F. Temple

A Roland Daniel Double: The Signal and The Return of Wu Fang — Classic thrillers from the 30s.

A Shot Rang Out — Three decades of reviews and articles by today's Anthony Boucher, Jon Breen. An essential book for any mystery lover's library.

A Smell of Smoke — A 1951 English countryside thriller by Miles Burton.

A Snark Selection — Lewis Carroll's *The Hunting of the Snark* with two Snarkian chapters by Harry Stephen Keeler — Illustrated by Gavin L. O'Keefe.

A Young Man's Heart — A forgotten early classic by Cornell Woolrich.

Alexander Laing Novels — *The Motives of Nicholas Holtz* and *Dr. Scarlett*, stories of medical mayhem and intrigue from the 30s.

An Angel in the Street — Modern hardboiled noir by Peter Genovese.

Automaton — Brilliant treatise on robotics: 1928-style! By H. Stafford Hatfield.

Away From the Here and Now — Clare Winger Harris stories, collected by Richard A. Lupoff

Beast or Man? — A 1930 novel of racism and horror by Sean M'Guire. Introduced by John Pelan.

Black Hogan Strikes Again — Australia's Peter Renwick pens a tale of the 30s outback.

Black River Falls — Suspense from the master, Ed Gorman.

Blondy's Boy Friend — A snappy 1930 story by Philip Wylie, writing as Leatrice Homesley.

Blood in a Snap — The *Finnegan's Wake* of the 21st century, by Jim Weiler.

Blood Moon — The first of the Robert Payne series by Ed Gorman.

Bogart '48 — Hollywood action with Bogie by John Stanley and Kenn Davis

Calling Lou Largo! — Two Lou Largo novels by William Ard.

Cornucopia of Crime — Francis M. Nevins assembled this huge collection of his writings about crime literature and the people who write it. Essential for any serious mystery library.

Corpse Without Flesh — Strange novel of forensics by George Bruce

Crimson Clown Novels — By Johnston McCulley, author of the Zorro novels, *The Crimson Clown* and *The Crimson Clown Again*.

Dago Red — 22 tales of dark suspense by Bill Pronzini.

Dark Sanctuary — Weird Menace story by H. B. Gregory

David Hume Novels — *Corpses Never Argue, Cemetery First Stop, Make Way for the Mourners, Eternity Here I Come*. 1930s British hardboiled fiction with an attitude.

Dead Man Talks Too Much — Hollywood boozer by Weed Dickenson.

Death Leaves No Card — One of the most unusual murdered-in-the-tub mysteries you'll ever read. By Miles Burton.

Death March of the Dancing Dolls and Other Stories — Volume Three in the Day Keene in the Detective Pulps series. Introduced by Bill Crider.

Deep Space and other Stories — A collection of SF gems by Richard A. Lupoff.

Detective Duff Unravels It — Episodic mysteries by Harvey O'Higgins.

Diabolic Candelabra — Classic 30s mystery by E.R. Punshon

Dime Novels: Ramble House's 10-Cent Books — *Knife in the Dark* by Robert Leslie Bellem, *Hot Lead* and *Song of Death* by Ed Earl Repp, *A Hashish House in New York* by H.H. Kane, and five more.

Don Diablo: Book of a Lost Film — Two-volume treatment of a western by Paul Landres, with diagrams. Intro by Francis M. Nevins.

Dope and Swastikas — Two strange novels from 1922 by Edmund Snell

Dope Tales #1 — Two dope-riddled classics; *Dope Runners* by Gerald Grantham and *Death Takes the Joystick* by Phillip Condé.

Dope Tales #2 — Two more narco-classics; *The Invisible Hand* by Rex Dark and *The Smokers of Hashish* by Norman Berrow.

Dope Tales #3 — Two enchanting novels of opium by the master, Sax Rohmer. *Dope* and *The Yellow Claw*.

Double Hot — Two 60s softcore sex novels by Morris Hershman.

Dr. Odin — Douglas Newton's 1933 racial potboiler comes back to life.

Evangelical Cockroach — Jack Woodford writes about writing.

Evidence in Blue — 1938 mystery by E. Charles Vivian.

Fatal Accident — Murder by automobile, a 1936 mystery by Cecil M. Wills.

Fighting Mad — Todd Robbins' 1922 novel about boxing and life

Finger-prints Never Lie — A 1939 classic detective novel by John G. Brandon.

Freaks and Fantasies — Eerie tales by Tod Robbins, collaborator of Tod Browning on the film FREAKS.

Gadsby — A lipogram (a novel without the letter E). Ernest Vincent Wright's last work, published in 1939 right before his death.

Gelett Burgess Novels — *The Master of Mysteries, The White Cat, Two O'Clock Courage, Ladies in Boxes, Find the Woman, The Heart Line, The Picaroons* and *Lady Mechante*. Recently added is A Gelett Burgess Sampler, edited by Alfred Jan. All are introduced by Richard A. Lupoff.

Geronimo — S. M. Barrett's 1905 autobiography of a noble American.

Hake Talbot Novels — *Rim of the Pit, The Hangman's Handyman.* Classic locked room mysteries, with mapback covers by Gavin O'Keefe.

Hands Out of Hell and Other Stories — John H. Knox's eerie hallucinations

Hell is a City — William Ard's masterpiece.

Hollywood Dreams — A novel of Tinsel Town and the Depression by Richard O'Brien.

Hostesses in Hell and Other Stories — Russell Gray's most graphic stories

House of the Restless Dead — Strange and ominous tales by Hugh B. Cave

I Stole $16,000,000 — A true story by cracksman Herbert E. Wilson.

Inclination to Murder — 1966 thriller by New Zealand's Harriet Hunter.

Invaders from the Dark — Classic werewolf tale from Greye La Spina.

J. Poindexter, Colored — Classic satirical black novel by Irvin S. Cobb.

Jack Mann Novels — Strange murder in the English countryside. *Gees' First Case, Nightmare Farm, Grey Shapes, The Ninth Life, The Glass Too Many, Her Ways Are Death, The Kleinert Case* and *Maker of Shadows.*

Jake Hardy — A lusty western tale from Wesley Tallant.

Jim Harmon Double Novels — *Vixen Hollow/Celluloid Scandal, The Man Who Made Maniacs/Silent Siren, Ape Rape/Wanton Witch, Sex Burns Like Fire/Twist Session, Sudden Lust/Passion Strip, Sin Unlimited/Harlot Master, Twilight Girls/Sex Institution.* Written in the early 60s and never reprinted until now.

Joel Townsley Rogers Novels and Short Stories — By the author of *The Red Right Hand: Once In a Red Moon, Lady With the Dice, The Stopped Clock, Never Leave My Bed.* Also two short story collections: *Night of Horror* and *Killing Time.*

John Carstairs, Space Detective — Arboreal Sci-fi by Frank Belknap Long

Joseph Shallit Novels — *The Case of the Billion Dollar Body, Lady Don't Die on My Doorstep, Kiss the Killer, Yell Bloody Murder, Take Your Last Look.* One of America's best 50's authors and a favorite of author Bill Pronzini.

Keller Memento — 45 short stories of the amazing and weird by Dr. David Keller.

Killer's Caress — Cary Moran's 1936 hardboiled thriller.

Lady of the Yellow Death and Other Stories — More stories by Wyatt Blassingame.

League of the Grateful Dead and Other Stories — Volume One in the Day Keene in the Detective Pulps series.

Library of Death — Ghastly tale by Ronald S. L. Harding, introduced by John Pelan

Malcolm Jameson Novels and Short Stories — *Astonishing! Astounding!, Tarnished Bomb, The Alien Envoy and Other Stories* and *The Chariots of San Fernando and Other Stories.* All introduced and edited by John Pelan or Richard A. Lupoff.

Man Out of Hell and Other Stories — Volume II of the John H. Knox weird pulps collection.

Marblehead: A Novel of H.P. Lovecraft — A long-lost masterpiece from Richard A. Lupoff. This is the "director's cut", the long version that has never been published before.

Master of Souls — Mark Hansom's 1937 shocker is introduced by weirdologist John Pelan.

Max Afford Novels — *Owl of Darkness, Death's Mannikins, Blood on His Hands, The Dead Are Blind, The Sheep and the Wolves, Sinners in Paradise* and *Two Locked Room Mysteries and a Ripping Yarn* by one of Australia's finest mystery novelists.

Money Brawl — Two books about the writing business by Jack Woodford and H. Bedford-Jones. Introduced by Richard A. Lupoff.

More Secret Adventures of Sherlock Holmes — Gary Lovisi's second collection of tales about the unknown sides of the great detective.

Muddled Mind: Complete Works of Ed Wood, Jr. — David Hayes and Hayden Davis deconstruct the life and works of the mad, but canny, genius.

Murder among the Nudists — A mystery from 1934 by Peter Hunt, featuring a naked Detective-Inspector going undercover in a nudist colony.

Murder in Black and White — 1931 classic tennis whodunit by Evelyn Elder.

Murder in Shawnee — Two novels of the Alleghenies by John Douglas: *Shawnee Alley Fire* and *Haunts*.

Murder in Silk — A 1937 Yellow Peril novel of the silk trade by Ralph Trevor.

My Deadly Angel — 1955 Cold War drama by John Chelton.

My First Time: The One Experience You Never Forget — Michael Birchwood — 64 true first-person narratives of how they lost it.

Mysterious Martin, the Master of Murder — Two versions of a strange 1912 novel by Tod Robbins about a man who writes books that can kill.

Norman Berrow Novels — *The Bishop's Sword, Ghost House, Don't Go Out After Dark, Claws of the Cougar, The Smokers of Hashish, The Secret Dancer, Don't Jump Mr. Boland!, The Footprints of Satan, Fingers for Ransom, The Three Tiers of Fantasy, The Spaniard's Thumb, The Eleventh Plague, Words Have Wings, One Thrilling Night, The Lady's in Danger, It Howls at Night, The Terror in the Fog, Oil Under the Window, Murder in the Melody, The Singing Room*. This is the complete Norman Berrow library of locked-room mysteries, several of which are masterpieces.

Old Faithful and Other Stories — SF classic tales by Raymond Z. Gallun

Old Times' Sake — Short stories by James Reasoner from Mike Shayne Magazine.

One Dreadful Night — A classic mystery by Ronald S. L. Harding

Pair O' Jacks — A mystery novel and a diatribe about publishing by Jack Woodford

Perfect .38 — Two early Timothy Dane novels by William Ard. More to come.

Prince Pax — Devilish intrigue by George Sylvester Viereck and Philip Eldridge

Prose Bowl — Futuristic satire of a world where hack writing has replaced football as our national obsession, by Bill Pronzini and Barry N. Malzberg.

Red Light — The history of legal prostitution in Shreveport Louisiana by Eric Brock. Includes wonderful photos of the houses and the ladies.

Researching American-Made Toy Soldiers — A 276-page collection of a lifetime of articles by toy soldier expert Richard O'Brien.

Reunion in Hell — Volume One of the John H. Knox series of weird stories from the pulps. Introduced by horror expert John Pelan.

Ripped from the Headlines! — The Jack the Ripper story as told in the newspaper articles in the *New York* and *London Times*.

Robert Randisi Novels — *No Exit to Brooklyn* and *The Dead of Brooklyn*. The first two Nick Delvecchio novels.

Rough Cut & New, Improved Murder — Ed Gorman's first two novels.

R.R. Ryan Novels — Freak Museum and The Subjugated Beast, two horror classics.

Ruled By Radio — 1925 futuristic novel by Robert L. Hadfield & Frank E. Farncombe.

Rupert Penny Novels — *Policeman's Holiday, Policeman's Evidence, Lucky Policeman, Policeman in Armour, Sealed Room Murder, Sweet Poison, The Talkative Policeman, She had to Have Gas* and *Cut and Run* (by Martin Tanner.) Rupert Penny is the pseudonym of Australian Charles Thornett, a master of the locked room, impossible crime plot.

Sacred Locomotive Flies — Richard A. Lupoff's psychedelic SF story.

Sam — Early gay novel by Lonnie Coleman.

Sand's Game — Spectacular hard-boiled noir from Ennis Willie, edited by Lynn Myers and Stephen Mertz, with contributions from Max Allan Collins, Bill Crider, Wayne Dundee, Bill Pronzini, Gary Lovisi and James Reasoner.

Sand's War — More violent fiction from the typewriter of Ennis Willie

Satan's Den Exposed — True crime in Truth or Consequences New Mexico — Award-winning journalism by the *Desert Journal*.

Satans of Saturn — Novellas from the pulps by Otis Adelbert Kline and E. H. Price

Satan's Sin House and Other Stories — Horrific gore by Wayne Rogers

Secrets of a Teenage Superhero — Graphic lit by Jonathan Sweet

Sex Slave — Potboiler of lust in the days of Cleopatra by Dion Leclerq, 1966.

Shadows' Edge — Two early novels by Wade Wright: *Shadows Don't Bleed* and *The Sharp Edge*.

Sideslip — 1968 SF masterpiece by Ted White and Dave Van Arnam.

Slammer Days — Two full-length prison memoirs: *Men into Beasts* (1952) by George Sylvester Viereck and *Home Away From Home* (1962) by Jack Woodford.

Slippery Staircase — 1930s whodunit from E.C.R. Lorac

Sorcerer's Chessmen — John Pelan introduces this 1939 classic by Mark Hansom.

Star Griffin — Michael Kurland's 1987 masterpiece of SF drollery is back.

Stakeout on Millennium Drive — Award-winning Indianapolis Noir by Ian Woollen.

Strands of the Web: Short Stories of Harry Stephen Keeler — Edited and Introduced by Fred Cleaver.

Summer Camp for Corpses and Other Stories — Weird Menace tales from Arthur Leo Zagat; introduced by John Pelan.

Suzy — A collection of comic strips by Richard O'Brien and Bob Vojtko from 1970.

Tales of the Macabre and Ordinary — Modern twisted horror by Chris Mikul, author of the *Bizarrism* series.

Tenebrae — Ernest G. Henham's 1898 horror tale brought back.

The Amorous Intrigues & Adventures of Aaron Burr — by Anonymous. Hot historical action about the man who almost became Emperor of Mexico.

The Anthony Boucher Chronicles — edited by Francis M. Nevins. Book reviews by Anthony Boucher written for the *San Francisco Chronicle,* 1942 – 1947. Essential and fascinating reading by the best book reviewer there ever was.

The Barclay Catalogs — Two essential books about toy soldier collecting by Richard O'Brien

The Basil Wells Omnibus — A collection of Wells' stories by Richard A. Lupoff.

The Beautiful Dead and Other Stories — Dreadful tales from Donald Dale

The Best of 10-Story Book — edited by Chris Mikul, over 35 stories from the literary magazine Harry Stephen Keeler edited.

The Black Dark Murders — Vintage 50s college murder yarn by Milt Ozaki, writing as Robert O. Saber.

The Book of Time — The classic novel by H.G. Wells is joined by sequels by Wells himself and three stories by Richard A. Lupoff. Illustrated by Gavin L. O'Keefe.

The Case in the Clinic — One of E.C.R. Lorac's finest.

The Case of the Bearded Bride — #4 in the Day Keene in the Detective Pulps series

The Case of the Little Green Men — Mack Reynolds wrote this love song to sci-fi fans back in 1951 and it's now back in print.

The Case of the Withered Hand — 1936 potboiler by John G. Brandon.

The Charlie Chaplin Murder Mystery — A 2004 tribute by noted film scholar, Wes D. Gehring.

The Chinese Jar Mystery — Murder in the manor by John Stephen Strange, 1934.

The Compleat Calhoon — All of Fender Tucker's works: Includes *Totah Six-Pack, Weed, Women and Song* and *Tales from the Tower,* plus a CD of all of his songs.

The Compleat Ova Hamlet — Parodies of SF authors by Richard A. Lupoff. This is a brand new edition with more stories and more illustrations by Trina Robbins.

The Contested Earth and Other SF Stories — A never-before published space opera and seven short stories by Jim Harmon.

The Crimson Query — A 1929 thriller from Arlton Eadie. A perfect way to get introduced.

The Curse of Cantire — Classic 1939 novel of a family curse by Walter S. Masterman.

The Devil and the C.I.D. — Odd diabolic mystery by E.C.R. Lorac

The Devil Drives — An odd prison and lost treasure novel from 1932 by Virgil Markham.

The Devil's Mistress — A 1915 Scottish gothic tale by J. W. Brodie-Innes, a member of Aleister Crowley's Golden Dawn.

The Devil's Nightclub and Other Stories — John Pelan introduces some gruesome tales by Nat Schachner.

The Disentanglers — Episodic intrigue at the turn of last century by Andrew Lang

The Dumpling — Political murder from 1907 by Coulson Kernahan.

The End of It All and Other Stories — Ed Gorman selected his favorite short stories for this huge collection.

The Fangs of Suet Pudding — A 1944 novel of the German invasion by Adams Farr

The Ghost of Gaston Revere — From 1935, a novel of life and beyond by Mark Hansom, introduced by John Pelan.

The Girl in the Dark — A thriller from Roland Daniel

The Gold Star Line — Seaboard adventure from L.T. Reade and Robert Eustace.

The Golden Dagger — 1951 Scotland Yard yarn by E. R. Punshon.

The Great Orme Terror — Horror stories by Garnett Radcliffe from the pulps

The Hairbreadth Escapes of Major Mendax — Francis Blake Crofton's 1889 boys' book.

The House That Time Forgot and Other Stories — Insane pulpitude by Robert F. Young

The House of the Vampire — 1907 poetic thriller by George S. Viereck.

The Illustrious Corpse — Murder hijinx from Tiffany Thayer

The Incredible Adventures of Rowland Hern — Intriguing 1928 impossible crimes by Nicholas Olde.

The Julius Caesar Murder Case — A classic 1935 re-telling of the assassination by Wallace Irwin that's much more fun than the Shakespeare version.

The Koky Comics — A collection of all of the 1978-1981 Sunday and daily comic strips by Richard O'Brien and Mort Gerberg, in two volumes.

The Lady of the Terraces — 1925 missing race adventure by E. Charles Vivian.

The Lord of Terror — 1925 mystery with master-criminal, Fantômas.

The Melamare Mystery — A classic 1929 Arsene Lupin mystery by Maurice Leblanc

The Man Who Was Secrett — Epic SF stories from John Brunner

The Man Without a Planet — Science fiction tales by Richard Wilson

The N. R. De Mexico Novels — Robert Bragg, the real N.R. de Mexico, presents *Marijuana Girl, Madman on a Drum, Private Chauffeur* in one volume.

The Night Remembers — A 1991 Jack Walsh mystery from Ed Gorman.

The One After Snelling — Kickass modern noir from Richard O'Brien.

The Organ Reader — A huge compilation of just about everything published in the 1971-1972 radical bay-area newspaper, *THE ORGAN*. A coffee table book that points out the shallowness of the coffee table mindset.

The Poker Club — Three in one! Ed Gorman's ground-breaking novel, the short story it was based upon, and the screenplay of the film made from it.

The Private Journal & Diary of John H. Surratt — The memoirs of the man who conspired to assassinate President Lincoln.

The Secret Adventures of Sherlock Holmes — Three Sherlockian pastiches by the Brooklyn author/publisher, Gary Lovisi.

The Shadow on the House — Mark Hansom's 1934 masterpiece of horror is introduced by John Pelan.

The Sign of the Scorpion — A 1935 Edmund Snell tale of oriental evil.

The Singular Problem of the Stygian House-Boat — Two classic tales by John Kendrick Bangs about the denizens of Hades.

The Smiling Corpse — Philip Wylie and Bernard Bergman's odd 1935 novel.

The Spider: Satan's Murder Machines — A thesis about Iron Man

The Stench of Death: An Odoriferous Omnibus by Jack Moskovitz — Two complete novels and two novellas from 60's sleaze author, Jack Moskovitz.

The Story Writer and Other Stories — Classic SF from Richard Wilson

The Strange Case of the Antlered Man — 1935 dementia from Edwy Searles Brooks

The Strange Thirteen — Richard B. Gamon's odd stories about Raj India.

The Technique of the Mystery Story — Carolyn Wells' tips about writing.

The Threat of Nostalgia — A collection of his most obscure stories by Jon Breen

The Time Armada — Fox B. Holden's 1953 SF gem.

The Tongueless Horror and Other Stories — Volume One of the series of short stories from the weird pulps by Wyatt Blassingame.

The Tracer of Lost Persons — From 1906, an episodic novel that became a hit radio series in the 30s. Introduced by Richard A. Lupoff.

The Trail of the Cloven Hoof — Diabolical horror from 1935 by Arlton Eadie. Introduced by John Pelan.

The Triune Man — Mindscrambling science fiction from Richard A. Lupoff.

The Unholy Goddess and Other Stories — Wyatt Blassingame's first DTP compilation

The Universal Holmes — Richard A. Lupoff's 2007 collection of five Holmesian pastiches and a recipe for giant rat stew.

The Werewolf vs the Vampire Woman — Hard to believe ultraviolence by either Arthur M. Scarm or Arthur M. Scram.

The Whistling Ancestors — A 1936 classic of weirdness by Richard E. Goddard and introduced by John Pelan.

The White Owl — A vintage thriller from Edmund Snell

The White Peril in the Far East — Sidney Lewis Gulick's 1905 indictment of the West and assurance that Japan would never attack the U.S.

The Wizard of Berner's Abbey — A 1935 horror gem written by Mark Hansom and introduced by John Pelan.

The Wonderful Wizard of Oz — by L. Frank Baum and illustrated by Gavin L. O'Keefe

Through the Looking Glass — Lewis Carroll wrote it; Gavin L. O'Keefe illustrated it.

Time Line — Ramble House artist Gavin O'Keefe selects his most evocative art inspired by the twisted literature he reads and designs.

Tiresias — Psychotic modern horror novel by Jonathan M. Sweet.

Totah Six-Pack — Fender Tucker's six tales about Farmington in one sleek volume.

Trail of the Spirit Warrior — Roger Haley's historical saga of life in the Indian Territories.

Two Kinds of Bad — Two 50s novels by William Ard about Danny Fontaine

Two Suns of Morcali and Other Stories — Evelyn E. Smith's SF tour-de-force

Ultra-Boiled — 23 gut-wrenching tales by our Man in Brooklyn, Gary Lovisi.

Up Front From Behind — A 2011 satire of Wall Street by James B. Kobak.

Victims & Villains — Intriguing Sherlockiana from Derham Groves.

Wade Wright Novels — *Echo of Fear, Death At Nostalgia Street, It Leads to Murder* and *Shadows' Edge*, a double book featuring *Shadows Don't Bleed* and *The Sharp Edge.*

Walter S. Masterman Novels — *The Green Toad, The Flying Beast, The Yellow Mistletoe, The Wrong Verdict, The Perjured Alibi, The Border Line, The Bloodhounds Bay* and *The Curse of Cantire.* Masterman wrote horror and mystery, some introduced by John Pelan.

We Are the Dead and Other Stories — Volume Two in the Day Keene in the Detective Pulps series, introduced by Ed Gorman. When done, there may be as many as 11 in the series.

Welsh Rarebit Tales — Charming stories from 1902 by Harle Oren Cummins

West Texas War and Other Western Stories — by Gary Lovisi.

Whip Dodge: Man Hunter — Wesley Tallant's saga of a bounty hunter of the old West.

Win, Place and Die! — The first new mystery by Milt Ozaki in decades. The ultimate novel of 70s Reno.

You'll Die Laughing — Bruce Elliott's 1945 novel of murder at a practical joker's English countryside manor.

RAMBLE HOUSE

Fender Tucker, Prop.   Gavin L. O'Keefe, Graphics
www.ramblehouse.com   fender@ramblehouse.com
228-826-1783   10329 Sheephead Drive, Vancleave MS 39565